GW00722599

The Accidental Tyrant

Amelie Woodford

Honeybee Books

Published by Honeybee Books
Broadoak, Dorset
www.honeybeebooks.co.uk

Cover Photo © 2014 Kerry Tate

Copyright © 2014 Amelie Woodford

The right of Amelie Woodford to be identified as the author
of this work has been asserted by her in accordance with
the Copyright, Design and Patents Act 1988.

9 780992 902933

To

E. F. P

Part One

Truth

✳

Darling, Esmella-

I am not proud of everything I have done in my life, but I believe you deserve to know the truth about your heritage. This is not information I can reveal whilst I am alive and you would be wise to keep it to yourself too. Feel free to add to it. One day, when our lives are but a distant memory, historians will use our words to piece together history.

I pray that after reading this, you will find it in your heart to forgive me for the secrets I have kept and understand that I always had our interests at heart.

Love always x x

Chapter One – The Catalyst

"Sir, I think you need to see this."

Malachi rushed over to my station. I pointed, speechless, to the blank screen before me. We both stood there staring expectantly, waiting for the steady flow of numbers to resume but nothing happened. Nervous whispers began to rise around us as other people found their data streams reporting the same findings: nothing. The usual chatter of the machinery was silenced and replaced with an intermittent beeping. It was eerie. In the whole time we had been monitoring Earth, we had never encounter anything like this.

"Malachi?"

Malachi may as well have been our commanding officer. He was by far the oldest amongst us, although we don't take much notice of age. He had eyes filled with pain, sorrow and wisdom. His skin was on the bluish side of silver; probably bluer than any other Holiterian's I had ever met.

We knew little about his background, as he was a very private man, yet we all trusted him with our lives. He was not just a great leader; he was an inspiration and confidante. So, in that time of confusion, all eyes were on him.

"Get me Josiah. Now!" he boomed.

Silence fell again as Josiah, the head of the engineering department, was ushered quickly towards us.

"Machinery stats?"

"Everything running correctly, sir." Josiah assured.

Malachi turned him aside from the rest of the room, "Josiah, could our position here have been compromised?"

Their voices were hushed, barely audible, yet the room around them was frozen as everyone waited with bated breath for the response.

"No, Malachi. We are confident that's not the case." he whispered, "There's data getting through, just not much. If they'd cut us off, we'd still be picking up normal areas of human activity and energy- it'd just be the wireless data that'd be stopped. Honestly, I think something's happened down there. Something bad."

Just like that, the room breathed again. The fear of being discovered was always high. The inhabitants of Earth had a record of violence and warfare, much like the history of our own planet, Holiteria. We couldn't guarantee our safety if they discovered us. Although a military branch, we did not have the fighting capabilities to go up against a whole planet. Everyone there knew that support was too far away to reach us in time. As a result there was an initial feeling of relief, before chaos ensued.

"Analysts." Malachi commanded our attention. "I want reports on all the data in the hour leading up to this."

I turned to my computer and other analysts did the same. Suddenly the room was alive as people typed furiously into their computers and barked verbal commands into their handhelds. Men began tapping into available surveillance equipment. Others were communicating the situation to leaders back in Holiteria. Malachi was collating information in a large holographic display at one end of the room. Everything accelerated as we desperately attempted to build up a complete image of the situation.

I was sat in the centre of a whirlwind. We had travelled throughout the solar universe to find other intelligent and thriving life forms. We had spent many rotations here on Venus observing

Earth. We were excited by our findings. Now it all seemed to be slipping away. I stared at the charts in front of me searching desperately for the answer. Numbers swam before my eyes. Nothing made sense.

My day had begun with the mundane task of scanning a computerised image showing high density areas of human life. We had been tracking changes and growth patterns for a long time, and change was always slow and steady. The last thing I expected to see was an energy explosion resonating across the screen, yet that's what happened: 520,334 kilotons of energy radiating out across Moscow. Then 519,950 kilotons centred on Washington. Next: London- Jerusalem- Bagdad- Tokyo- Sydney. The chain reaction had run in a green haze across my screen. The figures had been unprecedented. Now, as I prepared my report, I checked them over and over again, but they didn't change. That had really happened.

Now there was nothing. The figures flowing in were negligible. It was as if all the life on earth had been wiped away. Man, beast and plants all appeared to have been eradicated by whatever had caused the explosions. I felt a wave of nervous energy and kept glancing at the screen, waiting for it to burst back to life. Still nothing happened.

Josiah's voice pierced through my thoughts. An emergency meeting of the council had been called and even Abram, our true commanding officer, would be there. Abram demanded high standards and I, more than anyone, felt the need to prove myself, professionally, in front of him.

I walked to the conference room with the taste of panic in my mouth. As a woman in a misogynistic world, holding a position of power came with added responsibilities. I sat there flicking between the various pages projected in front of me from my handheld. I ran through my speech in my mind. I wanted to make sure that I was thoroughly prepared for any questions that might be thrown at me.

Growing up, even my mother had told me this was no job for a girl to aspire to; at the time, she was right. I was the first woman ever to be allowed to go to Venus Station. I would like to say that I got there on my own merit but unfortunately that isn't entirely true. The men were outraged. They couldn't see how they could work in such a perilous location with a woman, because they would be constantly distracted by their need to protect her. The higher ranking officers feared for my safety in a station full of sexually frustrated men on long deployments. I had nothing to worry about there. The day I arrived, Javari, who I had met briefly at my wedding, told me that he liked the way I was wearing my hair. Abram's reaction to that ensured that the men feared even talking to me from that moment forth. It made my existence very lonely.

So I went there- a revolutionary in my own right- and I succeeded. I helped pioneer a new method of data collection to measure energy output from the surface of the planet. I worked with men to secretly intercept all data that was being sent via wireless transmissions right across planet Earth. I helped to ensure that we had access to every piece of digital information that any person down there sent or received to anywhere else on their planet.

I made a huge impact and paved the way for the women who have since joined me in the ranks. Despite this, I felt like a fraud at times; I felt like womankind's entire position in this field was based on a weak foundation because I know Abram put me there. I needed to be outstanding in my work to demonstrate to myself and my male colleagues that I deserved my position.

In this meeting, I was under the scrutiny of all the highest-ranking men in the army. This was the time that I needed to get it right. I couldn't afford to slip up.

Josiah spoke first. He had been looking for answers from outside of Earth's atmosphere. He confirmed that no cosmic impacts had occurred that would account for the data. Malachi, Samson, Javari and I all offered equally unhelpful reports. Not one of us could find a concrete answer. I made the assumption, based on my data, that we were looking at the aftermath of a nuclear war. Animated conversation followed as the implications of this potential situation were explored. I was relieved that my idea was being taken seriously. I relaxed as the conversation flared up. My part was done. If this was nuclear war, the next course of action would fall on the strategists.

"Enough." Abram's voice rose up through the babble and was met with immediate silence. It is rare to find a man whose authority is such that he need barely say a word and the entire population jumps to hear it. He exudes power. Men fear and respect him. He never shouts; he is always in complete control- of himself and those around him.

My mind drifted back to a memory of the first time I laid eyes on him, back at home, at the rally. As he rose to the stand stillness wove its course around the crowd and, within a matter of seconds, conversation had ceased. All eyes were on him and every heart and mind was open to him, waiting for him to speak. They weren't disappointed.

Now, in the conference room, he spoke once again to an expectant crowd. "I have no time to sit and suffer fools. This conversation is clearly going nowhere and idle supposition is no use to me or anyone else."

My mind strayed from the room and I imagined what might happen next. As I thought, my gaze fell outside the window. A glorious rainbow formed in droplets of sulphuric acid and smiled at me through the window. It was beautiful, breaking through the vicious plumes of Mount Estela. I found it hard to understand how something that magnificent could appear in a landscape so fiery and unforgiving. I couldn't help but be in awe of these rare moments of beauty. They made life on this forsaken planet bearable.

Of course, I missed home and my family and I worried about them dreadfully. Luckily, since Abram and his rallies had taken down the corrupt Chi, I knew life was better. My people finally had a chance to reclaim their existence and build a better life. With science as my first love though, I knew that this was what I wanted to do- where I had to be.

Sometimes I still feared that the men might have been right about having women on Venus. I hated being stuck indoors all the time; I felt like a caged animal in that metal pod. Everywhere was shiny and clinical. Machines whirred incessantly. I longed for nature.

Even looking out the windows brought no real relief; they just showed a world so violent and intense, that even our Holiterian skins couldn't cope with it. Volcanoes shaped the landscape, throwing columns of ash into the sky at regular intervals. Molten lava would flow in rivers across the surface, eating into the ground as it cooled. Then another explosion would ripple through and the skyline would be reshaped, again.

Men became childish in these settings. They teased each other and spoke coarsely. Some looked at me with a hunger that made my skin crawl. They talked about the female body and what they missed. They described in vivid detail what they wanted to do to their women when they returned home. I knew I was safe. I was under Abram's protection. Other women who went there weren't in the same situation. Perhaps the officers were right to fear for them.

It crossed my mind that none of that would matter anymore though. No life on Earth meant no reason to be there monitoring it. Although I thought we might continue to watch it to see how it recovered, in all honesty I had no idea what would happen and my mind was in overdrive. I certainly didn't expect what came next.

Samson's voice brought me back to the room, "Atarah? You want to take Atarah!?"

"Yes" came Abram's cool reply. His voice was like steel, "Does anyone take issue with this?"

Silence.

"Then it's decided. Atarah and I will fly to Earth!"

My heart leapt into my mouth. "But that's years ahead of schedule. Are we really ready?" I stammered.

"Samson will work his men, along with Josiah's, around the clock and get us ready." He clocked him a cold, sharp stare. It was clear he had viewed Samson's question about me as a question of his judgement and authority. I feared that this would come back to him at some point. "At least with the results of current data from Earth we won't be likely to meet any resistance. Protection shouldn't be required."

"That said, Abram, with all due respect, I would feel happier if you were to take Javari with you." Malachi was a voice of experience and reason. I knew Abram wouldn't want Javari joining us, but I also knew that Malachi was the only person that Abram would listen to. If Malachi truly wanted it, then it was as good as done.

"Malachi, if you expect me to take him with us, then please don't expect him to return in one piece- if at all!" Abram's usual sarcastic wit caused a mixture of fear and anxiety around the room as they half believed his casual threat. Javari's face was a picture of whiteness and his eyes sank deep into their sockets. He had never meant to cross him.

"Samson," Abram's voice was like deep, dark water now. "The junior rating who's been responsible for cleaning out the sewage disposal system is suffering from sickness and diarrhoea. I'm going to need you to go down and sort it out for us today. I suggest you wear a mask and take some gloves."

Chapter Two – History with Abram

I think to understand what happened next, it is essential to understand Abram. To help you to understand Abram, all I can do is tell you my history with him because that is what I know.

The first time I met him, I was at a rally. It was still dark, but we were coming to the end, and a dusky haze was already beginning to fill up the west side of the horizon. The dark time had seemed unending and people were feeling bleak. Whilst there is always heat at home, the area of Holiteria which is hospitable has long periods of night as it rotates very slowly.

The people were miserable. Since Sandoz had seized power from his cousin, Chi Mayniah, in a bloody plot to place himself as Chi of Holiteria, life was tough for everyone. As Chi, Sandoz raised taxes; everyone was in financial difficulties and hundreds were left starving. He evicted the aristocracy, my family included, and reinstated his new advisors into their stately homes. He stepped on the poor and squeezed every last breath of life from his people.

Chi Sandoz inherited the Military Guide, Monetary Guide and Personal Guide from his cousin's rule. He was merciless: he executed them all in a public display of power and defiance. He was there to witness it. He sat above the execution area, staring down with dark, wild eyes. When the public failed to attend, he had soldiers drag them from their houses. He made men, women and children watch the bloody deaths of those three trusted advisors. I was just a child and it was the first time I had ever seen someone die. My mother tried to shield me from it as much as possible as we were pushed around in the crowd like animals at the market. I still heard the noise and saw the blood.

It sent a clear message to us all. Things had changed; we could get on with it, or meet the same fate as the Guides. We barely believed change was possible. Chi Mayniah had been a worthy and fair leader. He had led us though good times and filled the land with happiness. When Chi Sandoz seized power from him through his brutal slaughter, there was nothing anyone could do. Our ruling system had been the same way for hundreds of years. By our own laws, Sandoz was the next heir to power.

There had been cruel leaders before. Now, eight years into his reign, things were worse than they had ever been. People were left to die in the streets like animals. Holiterian's rarely got sick, yet the poor were finding themselves constantly disease ridden as he had raised the prices for vaccinations and medical treatments. Anyone who didn't follow Chi Sandoz's rules were executed. He was heavy handed and feared.

The people were disaffected. Our history had never seen political unrest like the situation unravelling at that time and a charismatic and influential leader was taking advantage of it. Chi Sandoz needed removing and someone was prepared to make that happen.

The campaign to oust him swelled, nameless and faceless. Had the plan failed, Abram, the initially unknown instigator, could have left it at that and slipped back, unnoticed. Nobody would have been any the wiser.

Abram was intelligent. It was not in his nature to fail. His campaign was strong and played on the emotions of a people who were ready for a revolution. It empowered them. It grew at the same time as the promise of light and it brought hope to the masses. We were grateful to be called together and for the first time, we felt we could make a difference. That is why we were all there; that night was to be his first address to the people. Our revolution was finally to get a face.

Regardless of the optimism in our hearts, rain was pummelling down in great lumps, splashing against the muddy floor. It oozed under our feet, squelching as we walked. We were all, rich or poor, caked in mud up to our knees. Not one person there cared about that. Our eyes were all transfixed to the front where a deep, red light shone on a hastily crafted stand.

Everyone knew why we were there but nobody knew who was leading this coup d'état, so the air was electric with speculation, hope and fear.

Then Abram rose to the podium. The lights turned white.

"My fellow countrymen- welcome! Today you have united. For this, I thank you. In being here, you have shown you understand the need for change. For this, I thank you. I have a vision of a better world. It is world in which we live together peacefully, a world in which the rich are not rich because they have trodden on the poor but because they have worked hard and deserve to be there. In my vision for the future I see the Councillors of the People working to ensure that this land is a place of happiness for everyone.

Throughout our history, revolutions have taken place. Some revolutions have been bloody yet I hope that we have come far enough to make the necessary changes without the drawing of blood. Trust me when I say that I most definitely believe our cause worthy enough to die for and that I know our men are manly enough to stomach it, but I hope we have come far enough through evolution and civilisation to first use our voices as our swords.

I do not just want to remove the Chi from power, no! To do that would be fruitless as there would again come a time when someone equally evil would come back to power. I want to do away with the whole institution. I propose, as some of you will have read, constructing a Council of the People. The Councillors will be there for you. You will elect them into their positions and every three years you will have the chance to remove them or reinstate them as you see fit.

I offer my own services to preside over this council until it is properly formed and promise to ensure fair and honest elections. Once the Council of the People is established and working for your benefit, I will then step back and continue to pursue my own career projects- I am, after all, a military man at heart.

I have been a soldier in Holiteria and have defended my Chis against attacks from the Myters. We defeated them and in return took their land. We now reside in all the habitable land on Holiteria and we are great.

With no other enemy to defeat, the new Chi has turned against his own- against you. This is not in accordance with the oath I took upon joining the army. I defend the people. I defend you!

I believe that today it is time for me to return to my origins- to the people. This is the hour in which I denounce my allegiance to the Chi and lead us, the people, to the better world of which we all dream.

To those of you still loyal to the Chi I ask you this- are you prepared to continue living as you are when Holiteria changes?

I am here because I love our Holiteria. I love our home. I love each of you. The Chi, who rules through force and demands unfair taxes, cannot say the same and he must be removed.

People of Holiteria! Are you with me?"

A cheer roared through the congregation. Not one person looked away from the mesmerising image before them. Abram looked strong, trustworthy and handsome on the podium and his words had resonated in the hearts and souls of every person to whom he spoke.

He had the most beautiful silvery grey skin I had ever seen; there wasn't even a hint of blue in it. His hair was the palest of blues. In spite of this, his eyes were so dark they were almost black; a coveted feature denoting strength. His frame was muscular beneath his red uniform, upon which row upon row of medals hung, and it was easy to imagine his beautiful, sculpted chest, the outline of which was just visible under his shirt. All of those things made him physically alluring, but it was something about his confidence that spoke to me that day; he was so dignified. In the naivety of my childhood- I fell in love with him.

So I sought him out. As he descended from the podium, shaking hands, surrounded by a throng of willing supporters, I pushed myself forward. I had always been headstrong but there was something about this man that made me even more brazen. With all the beauty of my youth and understanding of a man's heart, I locked eyes with him and then lowered them bashfully to the ground with a smile that I knew would win him over.

My arrogance was not so much that I believed I would be the only woman to catch his attention; however, it turned out that I was. And, from the very moment I caught it, I had his eye. There was fierceness in his possessiveness and without words he beckoned me to follow him that night. And I did.

He was as poised away from the crowds as he had been in front of them. He placed his hand on the small of my back and led me away from everyone as if it was something we did everyday – as if I was his lover and this was nothing out of the ordinary for us.

As we stepped into the hall, a beautiful wooden ocella sat, just waiting to be played. Somewhat akin to a piano, the ocella is one of the most expensive instruments in Holiteria; it takes years to learn to play it effectively and is known for creating the music of the upper classes. A vase of yellow flowers stood boldly on top, so perfectly arranged I doubt it would have dared leave a watermark on the dark brown wood beneath it.

He led me to a grand staircase that twisted round the wall to the right of the entrance hall. It was lined with photographs and paintings of regal men in military uniforms and I realised that this man came from a whole line of successful men. As was customary in our culture, there were no images of women. The role of the woman was, generally, to be behind the scenes, at the beck and call of the man. When the woman was particularly beautiful, as I was, we were to be taken out and displayed to the envious public. Although the gender divides remained, by this point in our history, there was a growing sense of discontent- particularly amongst the younger generation.

As well as the intimidating portraits, there was a charming stained glass window, backed with the most natural looking light source I had ever seen. I knew it must have been a considerable expense to install such natural sunlight into his home and it was such a welcome sight after the long darkness.

My parents brought a sunlight feature into our home but we could only afford to have one in one room. Here they appeared to be in every room, behind every window. Light streamed in as naturally as the real light did in the summer. The windows were beautiful and bore the coat of arms of Abram's family- another reminder that I was far out of my league here.

My family were wealthy, even after the ruin of the economy, but this was beyond the realms of my reality.

My feet clicked across the marble floor and I couldn't help but wonder why this man, clearly so well looked after by the Chi, should wish to overthrow him- he was either incredibly selfless or there was something in it for him. I wondered if I was being foolish. We hadn't yet said two words to each other and there he was leading me to his room. I was taking an incredible risk and I wasn't really sure what for.

I began to forget my thoughts as my mind became dizzy and my skin felt alive everywhere his hands made contact with me.

We glided up the stairs and I felt a fire run through me as he walked behind me with his enchanting eyes running wildly over my body. There was something primal about his desire for me and I loved it.

Every worry and concern I might have had slid from my thoughts as his hand glided, gently up my thigh, squeezing firmly as it grazed across my buttocks then sliding round to the front to pull me backwards, hard against his body. By the time we had reached his room, he had undone my dress and it slipped silently to the floor as we entered. He turned me towards him, in constant control, and kissed my lips with such passion and fervour that I melted right into him.

We spent that whole night together, the most luxuriously silky sheets I could ever imagine against my naked skin. Those sheets were the softest thing in the room; there was nothing tender between us, just lust and heat. He took me from behind, wrapped my long hair around his hand and pulled my head backwards so that he could lean down and kiss me. I bit on his lip just hard enough to taste his salty blood. He grabbed my wrists so tightly he left marks. We were animalistic in our passions but there was something else between us too. I felt a spark of light ignite that night.

That was the moment my life changed course forever.

I followed him everywhere. He gave me something special and I didn't feel like I was just an accessory, as a woman should be, because he listened to me and allowed me my dreams, which was something quite unheard of in our culture. He made me feel unique, loved and safe. My parents were overjoyed at the union. They hoped that it would offer me a future of stability.

We were coming together during a time of immense change in our homeland. The battle wasn't as blood-less as Abram had hoped. Those who opposed change, particularly those who had been favoured by the Chi, fought relentlessly. Unfortunately for them, Abram and his men had man power on their side and military training. Most of Abram's comrades had made the smooth transition from his ranks in the army to his guerrilla force.

Most of the time, I was kept separate from the fighting. We resided in the Chi's palace and lived a good life. Abram was reluctant to tell me the full extent of what was happening outside those gates for fear of upsetting me. In my eyes, he was a hero, there to be worshipped. I was unquestioning of his strategy; sure he would do the right thing. In hindsight, perhaps this wasn't so wise.

I sat there safely ensconced in my castle believing that I was a princess and champion of the people. I dreamed Abram's dream of a wonderful life for us all. Yet there I was, walled up in the Royal Wing, unaware of the plight of hundreds.

Just outside the grounds of my home, a bloody battle raged. Grown men fought alongside young boys. Slain bodies littered the streets and blood streamed through gutters. Weeping wives and mothers cleared the bodies. Their hearts broke over their deceased loved ones but their tears had dried up as they became hardened to the spoils of war.

Food became scarce. Hungry infants wept in their mother's arms and bellies ached. The pain and hunger left marks on the faces of the affected and an empty void stared from behind their eyes. There was only the faintest glimmer of hope within them that Abram could salvage this mess and restore harmony. They were right to hold onto their hope.

My family, in the East Wing, were happy and contented. My father, fighting alongside Abram, was as keen to keep my mother in the dark as Abram was for me.

What I hadn't realised at the time was that marriage was being discussed and neither man wanted to jeopardise that with the dirty truth. Although the ultimate decision of my marriage fell to my father and potential suitor, every father knew that a woman could make one's life unpleasant if she didn't approve of a match. Every suitor knew that a woman who didn't want to marry you could be difficult to keep in her place. With this in mind, it was important both my mother and I were kept from knowing how the revolution had taken place.

Our family had been rich, powerful, advisors to the previous monarchy before Chi Sandoz had usurped the crown. We were then banished; though at least we had lived well as we had clung to our money in exile.

There were many Holiterians who still championed us from Chi Mayniah's days, so it made sense for us to be in union with the man who was going to remove Sandoz and restore harmony to the people.

I sometimes wonder if Abram had known who I was when he first saw me. I find it hard to believe that he would have bedded me without knowing my entire personal history first. Perhaps he did.

Perhaps this was why our bond changed once he knew I was in love with him. They say all relationships that begin ferociously find that the fire dies quickly. Abram always told me he loved me more than life itself. He told me he would die for me. We made love as intensely as we had that very first time. Yet it evolved from the relationship of equals that I believed we had had, to me being controlled, confronted with jealousy and feeling overprotected. I had no room to manoeuvre and quickly lost my sense of self.

The fascinating thing was that he gave me the illusion of choice. He manipulated me to ensure that what I wanted to do was exactly what he wanted me to do. He was a clever man. His speeches charmed the masses and catapulted him into their favour, as his words to me captivated me into believing that Abram's was the only right way. On top of this, he treated me well. He would buy me presents.

One day he came home with a deep gash across the side of his stomach that was being held together by a neat row of ten black stitches. There was still blood caked onto his sliced jacket. On seeing him, I fell to him and cried.

"What happened?" I exclaimed as the colour drained away from my cheeks.

"It's nothing, honestly. Just a scratch." He saw my eyes searching him for answers. "One of the loyalists jumped me on the way home." He added reluctantly. He seemed embarrassed to admit it as much as he was angry it had happened.

He saw the worry in my eyes.

"Don't fret about it, Atarah. You're a worrier but I'm a warrior!" he flashed me the biggest grin and flexed his muscles. We both began to laugh and he pulled me tight to him. I felt him wince with the pain of his wound but I wasn't going to take this moment from him. Finally, he put his hands on my shoulders and held me so he could look at me.

"I knew you'd be upset... That's why I didn't come home empty handed." He was beaming now, "I got you something. It'll remind you that I'm resilient and will always return to you."

He pulled a small box from his pocket. Inside was the most beautiful lip ring I had ever seen.

As was customary, when a girl reaches an age of maturity and her father is ready to see her married, she gets her lip pierced with a small gold stud. This way a potential suitor will know she is ready. When a man claims a woman as his wife, he offers her a piece of jewellery to wear through her lip. This is a sign to the world that this woman is loved and shows she is unavailable. The more extravagant the piece, the more wealthy her husband is. This stud was extravagant. Mounted on it was the largest, most dazzling gem I had ever seen.

"Abe... is this...?"

"Of course it is. You know how I feel for you. I want to show the whole world that I love you and you're mine. What do you think?"

"Yes," I squealed, "I love you too- with all my heart. Nothing would make me happier than to be your wife."

I was happy at that time. My mother and I spent hours arranging a magnificent wedding ceremony. It was to take place at the palace in the service room where all religious events were celebrated. We arranged for all the dignitaries to attend.

The next few months passed in a flurry of fancy meals as different chefs arrived to give us samples of their best dishes that we might choose for the wedding dinner. We ate elaborately served fruits, succulent meats and delectable sauces. Rare game was served to us on crystal plates. The service was impeccable as every man fought to win the exclusive rights to cater our reception. It was a great honour and one that would form the highlight of their career if it were to be bestowed upon them.

As well as this, there were dresses to choose. I chose a fashionable, knee length skirt in a delicate powder blue encrusted with blue gemstones. A matching band was chosen to bind around my breasts and it was carefully wrapped in a net overlay. On my bare midriff, a beautiful belt of brilliant clear gemstones clung together in floral patterns. My hair fell about my shoulders in soft, silvery white curls, adorned with sparkling jewels.

This wasn't the first ensemble I tried though. My mother and I had attended meetings with what seemed like a never ending list of dress-makers. Each one pulled me around as they measured me and tugged materials around me as I stood there on a small stand. It was tiresome and I was hot and exhausted. Each designer had a similar idea and it was all getting very tedious. When Shallimi arrived offering a different concept, I was relieved. I loved what she was suggesting and commissioned her to make my dress.

I didn't regret my decision. My mother cried when she saw me dressed that morning and even my father choked up with pride. Everyone gasped and exclaimed how beautiful they thought I looked. I walked on air all day.

It was a traditional and dignified service. I waited inside a circle of family and friends whilst Abram walked around the outside. As he reached where my mother and father were holding hands, they let go and moved back to let him in. Abram then came towards me and asked me if I would agree to be his wife for now and eternity. I looked demurely through my eyelashes and told him I would. I removed my gold lip stud, handed it to my father and turned back to Abram. He slipped the ring through my lip, picked me up and carried me up to the lake. Once there, the final part of the ceremony involved just the two of us.

We slipped out of our clothes, walked into the lake separately to symbolically wash away our past connections, and emerged together, hand in hand as husband and wife.

It was as simple as that.

By the time we returned, the second course of dinner was already being served. There was laughter and animated conversation. The tables were set out in long rows, decorated with a bright array of flowers and elegant crystal centrepieces. We made our way to the seats at the head of the main table and I took my place at Abram's side while our guests clapped and cheered our return to the party. Once the meal was over, we danced until our feet ached and our eyes were heavy. Eventually, the guests began to dissipate and soon it was just Abram and I that remained.

Once I was his officially, Abram pulled the reins in a little tighter.

The saving grace for me was his self-arranged mission to observe and analyse Earth, now possible in the stability forged by the Council of the People. He went without me, but his jealousy drove him crazy. He couldn't bear the thought of me being left behind where he couldn't keep an eye on me. He knew it was my dream to pursue a career in science and so he arranged for me to come to join him at the station on Venus. Even Abram wasn't in the position to be allowed to bring a civilian onto the base so it would have never been possible for me to arrive there solely to be his wife.

Although I could never do it, I had begun to wish there was a way to end our relationship. In youth, even the smartest woman can be bowled over by a powerful man. As much as I wanted to leave him, I was his wife and for that reason, I didn't feel I could. Truth be told, there were many advantages to being on his arm.

Chapter Three – Arrival on the Blue Planet

We had never entered an atmosphere quite like Earth's before, so the plan was for us to hover just outside it whilst we sent a small shuttle droid down to explore. Once we were satisfied that a safe landing had taken place, we were to follow behind.

The mission started well. The shuttle was deployed from our passenger craft and, with a powerful blast, was propelled into the gravitational field. Our calculations appeared promising. The force of gravity was offset to a good level by the air resistance created by the design of the shuttle.

The shuttle had a blunt body design which Josiah and his engineers had assured us would create a shockwave that would keep the intense heat away from the body itself. Insulation also played a part to absorb some of the heat. It was a miniature replica of the craft we were sat in.

We watched it plummet through the blue as a white streak, getting smaller and smaller. Abram was maintaining contact with it through transmissions sent to our own craft. It was giving us an automated commentary of its descent which appeared on a screen in front of us: "passing through atmosphere. Veloci-". It stopped. We had lost contact with it. If we couldn't safely land a shuttle we would never receive clearance to land ourselves.

I felt panic-stricken. The idea of being thrust through 3000 degree heat and being subjected to intense force petrified me. Abram got increasingly angry beside me. He threw his fist against the windows and began to yell. His fury increased my anxiety. He was desperate to make this journey. I was worried he might proceed with it regardless of whether we could land the shuttle.

The transmitter crackled and we all drew silent. All I could hear was the fast paced breathing of apprehension.

"Abram, I think it's time to call it a day," Malachi's voice sounded over our radio system.

"One more minute."

The minute crawled by. We were just about to give up hope altogether when our transmitter burst back to life with the shuttles robotic countdown to its physical landing on earth – "4" it crackled again and a second pause in transmission left us sitting in suspense "2- 1- Landing sequence deployed. Shuttle landed safely. Communication over."

Abram and Javari breathed a sigh of relief. I held my breath because I knew what was coming next. We had to take that perilous journey ourselves.

We all moved to our seats. I had entered into the atmospheres of different planets but we had been told this one would be unlike any that we had experienced before. Javari handed us our thermo-regulator suits to put on. Abram checked my seatbelt was fastened securely. Both men flicked several different switches on the complicated looking control panel.

"Ready?" Abram asked giving me a wink.

"I guess so..."

"Let's do this then!"

Suddenly we were being forced forward and our whole craft began to shake. I tried to turn my head to look at Abram for reassurance but it felt as if I was frozen as different forces played with my body and held me fast to one spot. I was at the mercy of the craft and fate.

The temperature began to heat up. We were a blazing inferno flying through the skies. Reds and oranges burned brightly outside my window and beads of sweat began to form on my head. Even inside my thermo-regulator suit I felt it. I began to panic. These suits were supposed to be invincible. If I could feel the heat now, what was to stop us being burnt alive? I began to fear we would be incinerated before we even reached the planet. My breathing increased rapidly and my stomach lurched.

Droplets of water appeared over the control panel and windows and ceilings. Little splashes fell down on me.

I felt hot and dizzy. I wanted to scream but I couldn't even open my mouth.

But then it began to ease off. Our velocity reduced as the atmosphere around us became thicker increasing the air resistance. Abram spun back into action and took manual control of the shuttle. I felt safe again and began to regain control of my breathing.

We were approaching the land at lightning speeds but I trusted Abram entirely and I knew we were going to be alright. He didn't fail me. We landed on that planet like a feather drifting to the ground.

We stepped out of our craft into a world of black. There were gradual sweeping hills, reaching up high above us. It looked like it should have been beautiful, except there were areas where great chunks had been bitten from the landscape and everything was coated in a smouldering dust. Behind us there was a vast expanse of sea at the bottom of sheer white cliffs; the whiteness of the chalk shone out where the outer edges had been ripped away and thrown into the unforgiving water. There was something menacing about that virginal, whiteness. Then there was the water... it was filled with blackened debris and shook and rocked as if the Creator himself had stirred it up wildly.

A rough road, littered with debris, ran parallel to the cliffs and, in places, simply fell away into the sea where chunks of the cliff had plummeted into the water below. Cracked as if the earth had been shaken to its very core, there were remnants of metal vehicles that had clearly been thrown from it. Everything was blackened with smoke and fire- except those sheer, white cliffs.

The landscape was dramatic. I imagined it would have been so anyway, but now that it had been pulled apart and burnt down, it was even more so. The land was coated in darkness as if it were night time; the only difference was the brilliant sunlight that streamed down. By the time we arrived, the thick, black smoke from the explosions had almost entirely disappeared. Everything here had ended and the universe, in its infinite wisdom, was continuing the way it always does.

I still hear that silence. Even with the waves licking their wounds below and the gentle breeze turning through the wreckage above, the silence was eerie. There were none of the beautiful sounds I had imagined; not the songs of birds, no buzz of conversation, or hum of traffic.

I felt a flutter of disappointment wash over me. In all my years studying this planet from afar, I had been in awe of the poetry, songs, videos, paintings, the artistic beauty that individuals were able to capture and that the development of human internet was able to transmit to us. These were the things I had hoped to see if I ever had the good grace and fortune to come to Earth.

Earth had seemed like such an inspired place. It was in stark contrast to Holiteria and I envied its inhabitants. They weren't subject to the long periods of darkness that we endured at home. Their planet had far greater areas that were hospitable than our own. I viewed this world as a superior one. I saw it as a place that, although not quite as technologically developed as our world on Holiteria, was far more exceptional in the area that mattered the most: natural beauty. I suppose I, like many others, had put it on a pedestal.

Back at home, the extreme heat meant that there were vast areas so uninhabitable that even bacteria struggled to grow. Great Plains, glowing orange, rolled endlessly, as far as the eye could see. In those areas, the only end from the relentlessly arid conditions was death. For many years, men who set out to explore it never returned. We built crafts to go across it, crafts that withstood volcanic heat. Crafts that took us as close to our sun as we thought possible- but there was something out there, something in the atmosphere, that caused even these strongest metals to crumble like sugar cubes. It become the source of a great many myths and legends in our culture.

Even our skins, evolved to deal with the blistering heat of our planet and the high levels of radiation in our atmosphere, could not survive out there in the wastelands. All we knew of it were the beautiful views from the top of Mount Illyria; the far stretching ocean of orange, reaching to a sky of dusky pinks and tangerine with rivers of purples and blues flowing through them, glistening with a glorious array of stars, twinkling as they burnt ferociously, light years away.

Eventually, as our technology developed, we found ways in. The whole area was barren. We searched it extensively and found nothing. It was technology created to explore the wastelands that paved our way for interstellar travel. Our physicists developed faster-than-light travel. Unlike earth, which takes its power from dead plant life, the Holiterian Solar Manipulation Team found a way to harness energy from the manipulation of solar flares. This gave us the energy output needed to thrust our way into the universe. We have a lot to thank the wastelands for.

This desert covered a vast area of Holiteria. Where life dwelled, the habitat was much more hospitable; although still harsh by the standards of the planet I found myself on- even in its state of disrepair.

My homeland was filled with lush forests. Trees of turquoise and jade reached up into the skies and filled our air with beautiful, life-giving oxygen. Warmth swum around us, hot by Earth standards, and it was constantly humid. Flowers thrived in the hot, moist air and beautiful posies of pinks and yellows grew freely around us and filled our homes. The brightness of those flowers made life a little more bearable in the long, endless nights. The sweet scent of them lingered long after the petals were gone and offered the deliciously saccharine aroma of heaven.

Darkness filled our lives for as long as the people on Earth would call a year. We suffered through these nights. Whilst the trees and flowers had grown throughout time to maintain their reserves to keep flourishing during this darkness, for the people and animals, life was harder. Our bodies worked on a semi-shutdown during these months. In spite of millions of years of evolution, suicide rates were high and people were unsettled.

On the other side of this coin, endless day can take its toll in just the same way. So we learnt to adapt to it artificially. We built our homes elaborately to enable us to give ourselves sunlight substitutes during the dark and with thick shutters to keep out the sun during the light periods. Our homes were richly designed and furnished- for those who could afford them to be. For those that couldn't, life was just that little bit harder. I hoped that now, things would be better for everyone.

It had always amazed me as I had come to know Earth how two planets so far apart, could have raised two species so similar. Yes, our pigmentation was very different but our basic structure was the same. We had slightly different contours on our faces but we made ourselves up in similar ways. Our lifestyles shared striking resemblances too. The only thing we seemed to have that was different to this planet I now stood on was respect. We loved and respected our planet, even if we didn't extend that courtesy to each other. The more I looked at this Earth, the more I realised that the inhabitants of it had taken it for granted; the creator had given them everything they could need and desire, everything to have an easy existence, and they had destroyed it and been unable to see how good it was.

"What have they done to themselves?!" Javari's voice broke through my thoughts as a feeling of sorrow washed over me.

"I'm sorry" I stammered, "I know it's crazy to grieve for something you never really knew."

Abram put his arm tenderly around my shoulder. I would have taken comfort in it, except I saw his sly sideways wink at Javari. I shrugged him off, picked up the digital transmitter and suggested we all get to work.

This area had clearly been at the very centre of a blast so we knew we were safe. There was no chance of life here. It seemed like an unlikely location to be targeted by the explosions, but we didn't complain as it worked well in our favour.

Abram went off to the west towards a building that looked as if it might, at least partly, still be intact. I told him I was going to head south and make my way down to the beach to see what could be gleaned from investigation there. Javari was going to head north to climb the hills and find a vantage point.

As I was collecting the equipment I needed, in a courageous move, Javari put his hand on my shoulder and gave it a gentle squeeze, "I feel that sense of loss too. I had high hopes for this planet." As he moved his arm, the soothing smell of the clocoli flower caught in my nostrils. It reminded me of a place I used to hide when I was little if I wanted some time away from everything. A clocoli flower grew right next to the entrance to the small parting amongst the bushes where I could conceal myself for a few moments. It reminded me that I could feel safe.

"Thank you" I mumbled, very aware I was blushing.

It was a perilous scramble to the shoreline. Large areas of the cliffs had simply slid down into the water. From what I could gather at this point, the cliffs were comprised of sands from different ages, slippery clay-like substances, rocks and fossils. If I had to guess, I would have said that the cliffs had probably been slipping down into the water long before this had happened here. It didn't make my descent any easier though.

I descended one foot at a time, feeling my way down to find a ledge or hole that I could use as a step. Rocks jutted out from the clay in some places and I was able to use these to help me clamber down. I was about half way down the cliff when I lost my footing as one of those rocks came away from the clay that was gripping it. I slid down grabbing at handfuls of rock and dirt trying to steady myself. I landed, with broken pride, at the bottom. I was dirty and scratched and dreading having to go back and tell the others what had happened. The last thing I wanted was for them to feel the need to wrap me up now I was here. Perhaps I wasn't entirely here on my own merit but I loved this- this was the career I had dreamed of and I wasn't going to let them take that from me.

I was at the bottom of the cliff. It was where I wanted to be and I was able to collect samples of everything I needed for testing. Water, stones, sand, floating debris. I was feeling pleased with my progress; then suddenly, I saw it. The waves were carrying something and they were pushing it towards the land, towards me. It took me a while to distinguish it from all the other debris, but as it came closer it was unmistakable. I was looking at a human. A dead human, but a human nonetheless. My initial reaction was to scream and I don't know whether that was from fear or shock. When I calmed down, I looked more closely at the charred figure.

As I explained already, they really weren't so different to us. Their basic shape and anatomy was the same anyway. They lacked the protective skin we had; in photos, their skin looked various shades of brown and beiges whereas ours were thicker and ranged from silver through to pale blue. Their hair was different too-shades of reds and blacks and browns. We had silvers, blues and brilliant white hair. Not that I could make out the skin tone or hair colour of these tattered remains that were wallowing in the surf. I felt close to this body. I could picture this wreckage as myself.

There was something strange about seeing a person here, blistered and pained, when most of the other traces of life had been blown into oblivion. I couldn't bear to leave it there though. I knew very little of the customs for the preparation of the dead here on Earth but I recalled reading that they bury them, deep in the ground. So I began to dig. Spurred on by my disappointments on this planet, fear of Abram, sorrow at the loss of this life and the worries about what would happen next, I dug a deep hole with just my bare hands.

The sand began to grind away at my skin and rip at my nails. We are a strong and fast race and I worked with a frenzied speed and power. The pain was excruciating but my skin was tough and it didn't take long to have a hole deep enough.

I waded slowly into the water and sang the funeral song native to my land:

> *Do not feel sorrow, just feel glad,*
> *This soul here doesn't want you sad,*
> *For they have gone to eternal life,*
> *It's you that's left to face the strife.*
> *So creator bless him, but creator bless me,*
> *And keep us with you for eternity.*

I wasn't sure whether religion counted for anything here, but in our culture it was important and I hated to give this poor body a burial without repose for its soul too.

My hands were scratched by the rocks and the sand, grazes and cuts were etched into them and they throbbed painfully. My lower half was dripping with the brine of the ocean, salty tears streamed down my cheeks and I let my hair fall, bedraggled, around my face as I heaved the body to the grave.

Before pushing it in, I forcefully ripped a nail from one of the fingers. It was a grim job but I knew I had to take something back with me that wouldn't raise suspicion about the location of a corpse. The body fought to hold on to it and I had to use all of the strength I had to prise it away. Vomit rose in my throat but I did it. Then, with one dirty nail in my hand, I rolled the cadaver into the ground.

I knelt for a long time staring into the hole. I worked methodically to use my arms to push the sand and rocks back into the hole. They thudded down onto the body and I felt numb. By the time the task was completed, I could barely recall how I had done it. I collapsed into a dishevelled heap on top of the mound that was the only remaining sign of what had happened. Slowly, I began to collect myself again and I rushed around to get back on with my work. The last thing that I wanted was for Abram, or Javari, to find out what I had done. I knew that the expectation of finding a body would be to bring it back for analysis. I just couldn't bring myself to do that this time. I had a fingernail and would say I found it on the beach. That would have to suffice.

Before I headed back to base, I had to finish the job I had come to do. My last task was to collect samples to check for microorganisms. Our immune system was finely tuned to our own planet and we had very little knowledge of what we might encounter here that could affect our health. The information from the microorganisms would then all be reported back to the biomedical staff at Venus Station.

We all came together again a few hours later. Abram and Javari had arrived back first. As I walked towards them I realised that Abram, who had his back to me, had Javari by the throat. I couldn't hear his words as I ran towards them. I faltered. I had no business to interfere in Abram's affairs. I kept moving forward cautiously.

As I got closer I could hear Abram snarling at him, "Remember I am your superior. I pay your wages. So keep your hands off her!"

Javari couldn't breathe. I stood there shocked. Abram became aware of my presence and let go of Javari, throwing him backwards as he coughed and spluttered trying to get air into his lungs.

"What was that about?" I asked once Javari had walked away a little.

"Nothing you need worry your pretty head about," he told me, condescendingly.

"Well, I hope it wasn't about me? Because you should know you have nothing to worry about from me."

"You aren't the one that concerns me!" He said crossly.

"Javari's not stupid enough to cross you, honey. We need to work here together for now- it is just the three of us after all." I tried to pacify him, very aware that he was in a horrible mood. "Let's not fight. We need to have a meeting shortly to share our findings from today."

"I know. You're right," he conceded and then added, "It's only because I love you so much."

"I love you too."

I took him by the arm and we walked over to where Javari was sitting trying to recover. He rubbed his neck when he saw us and then got to his feet. Abram offered him no apology and I am sure he expected none.

We moved swiftly onto business and settled down together to see what we had discovered in our initial investigations here. The one finding we all had was the high radiation readings. Other than that, there was not a lot remaining here to be seen or analysed. We had arrived in what appeared to be the epicentre of one of the explosions. Abram had communicated this information back to Venus Station along with the data of my report.

The one thing none of us had managed to find was any trace of living human or animal existence. Whatever happened here seemed to have terminated absolutely everything in sight. The only evidence that remained of any life was the burnt out tree stumps and charred remains of livestock and people, coupled with a bitter smell of death that lingered in the air and filled our nostrils with every waft of the breeze.

I kept my secret burial deep in my heart. I knew it wouldn't be possible to offer a ceremony to everybody that we discovered but, by maintaining the memory of this one as my own, it could remain my tribute.

Chapter Four- Resilience of Life

We had been on the planet for a month. A vast volume of data was collected and samples teleported to Venus for examination. I sometimes wished that we could teleport people too so that I could go home and see my family. Nobody had found a way to do that yet though as there was always some damage to molecular integrity in the teleportation process. It wasn't a problem for inanimate objects but living things always came through irreversibly changed; physically they appeared almost completely the same- the damage occurred on a different level that we didn't understand. It was too high of a risk. Maybe one day.

We set up residence in an old building that remained largely intact. It wasn't a grand home but it stood in a good location with an open view of the surrounding country. I imagine in its day it had been a castle or fortification of some type.

Sometimes I fancied I could see the soldiers, marching around the perimeter, firing guns from the wall, raising a bridge over a moat, which I pictured filled with water. It was easier for me to imagine the world as it had been than see it as it now was: a lifeless shell filled solely with memories. In this same way, when I thought of my life, I thought of my childhood. I loved my work but I didn't like who I was. This devastated world seemed to be a metaphor for my life. I had spent years dreaming of being here and now that I was, it wasn't everything I had hoped it would be.

The walls of the castle were built of solid stone. It wasn't warm though. The nuclear explosions had lowered the temperatures significantly. The smoke had disappeared before our arrival but the nuclear winter raged on. We were suffering in the cold

The Accidental Tyrant

temperatures and it was tough, especially as most sources of fuel had been demolished before we arrived so there was nothing much around to burn. We built fires where we could and dressed up in coats of fur brought from our home planet.

Each evening, the three of us would sit together. We eventually began to relax into the mission, after the icy start. Abram usually guided the conversation and we normally talked about work.

One evening, we were all sat outside, looking up at the stars. I had sat on a blanket on the ground, warmly wrapped in Holiterian furs, knees pulled tightly to my chest, gazing up at the stars. Abram reached across to stroke my long hair and told me he loved how it was sparkling silver in the light of the Earth's moon which was almost full that night. The sky was so clear, I dreamed I could almost see home, winking down at me from among millions of stars.

Abram was next to me, half lying on the ground. His head was held high and his eyes were glowing yet he looked peaceful and lost in thought. He reminded me of how he had been when we had first fallen in love. He looked young and full of dreams and promise. It was the first time in a very long time that I had looked at him and thought how handsome he was. I leaned into him and rested my head on his lap, sliding my hand under his jumper and tracing my fingers along the line of his scar on his side. As he played gently with a strand of my hair, I closed my eyes and fell asleep. I felt so safe and tranquil.

Javari had been sitting opposite us when I had drifted off. Somewhere between me falling asleep and Abram waking me up to move inside, he had gone back into the castle.

Abram and I made love that night with a tenderness I hadn't felt from him before.

I couldn't pinpoint the exact moment that it happened, but slowly the weather began to warm. We had calculated that the average temperatures here had dropped by several degrees across the planet but the sun began to shine more brightly and the temperature began to rise; it wasn't warm, but it was better.

And then buds started to rise up through the blackened earth.

They came through slowly at first. Little pinprick heads, bowed down towards the earth, pushed up through the surface and sought out the sun. They were vibrant shades of green and very much alive. Soon they came through thicker and faster. Yellow flowers began to appear, along with pinks, blues, whites and purples. Flowers sprouted everywhere. Colours emerged filling the dead earth and hope returned to the soil again. Weeds sprouted up where buildings had stood; bind weed crawled over the ruins of walls and fences as if it was trying to bandage their wounds.

In the face of crippling adversity, nature prevailed. In the planet's moment of need, new life thrust forward. Soft rains fell to water the plants. The flowers turned and opened themselves up to the streaming sunshine. Once again the beauty I had dreamed about was returning to this place. It filled me with hope.

Life was good with Abram too. He was excited to be there and spent most of his time out searching and exploring the land we had arrived on.

It became apparent it was a relatively small island. It was diamond shaped and, upon research, Abram had informed us that it was only 20 miles across. The whole island had been devastated but now that life was beginning to spring forward again, I could see that this had probably been an outstandingly beautiful place.

With Abram out for long stretches of time collecting evidence, my job was to analyse his findings and communicate with everyone back at the Station. Javari's job was security and, as it turned out, there was very little need for him to be there. I was incredibly grateful for his company though. We began to spend long stretches of time talking and became good friends.

I think we all became complacent. I genuinely believed things were looking up for me, as well as this planet.

Javari and I spent much of the day talking. I told him about my history with Abram and he listened- without judgement. It was the first time I had found someone to talk to freely. He was always reluctant to talk about himself though. That was until the day Abram came home and found us laughing and chatting.

I don't remember what we were laughing about anymore.

He came in through the door and we were in the hallway. I was about to walk upstairs to the communications room and Javari was about to go and sort out something for us to eat. We had a passing moment of laughter as our paths crossed and this was the moment he came in.

"Well this looks cosy," he sneered, "Javari, I thought I warned you to back off? Would you care to share the joke?"

"It was nothing- really," I told him, earnestly.

Clearly he did not believe me. He demanded that one of us tell him what we had been laughing at and Javari made an attempt to explain it to him.

"Really? You expect me to believe that this intimate little get together was about that? What sort of a person do you take me for?" His face was ashen by that point. His eyes were glowing. Before I realised what was happening, he grabbed my hand and enveloped it in his entire fist, squeezing hard. "Are you going to tell me?" He snarled, "Or am I going to break your hand?"

"We're telling the truth." I pleaded with him, "Please, Abe, you have to believe me. I love you! There's nothing going. You're the only man in my life."

"Seriously, let her go. If you have a problem, you can take it up with me" Javari sounded much more confident than I think he felt at that point, committing what he must have known would be suicide.

But miraculously, it worked. Abram pushed me to the floor and left me there, weeping.

"Have her" he spat venomously. Then he left.

Once the door had closed I realised I had been holding my breath. I inhaled, exhaled and then let Javari help me up from the floor. I found myself apologising for myself, for Abram, for the whole mess.

He told me I had no reason to apologise. Then he opened up to me about his life back on Holiteria for the first time.

He had come to Venus because he had been running away. He had been with his childhood sweetheart, Marelli, since school. They had grown up together and their parents had always joked they would be together forever. They had come to think so too. He told me stories of long walks through the darkness together- holding hands and just talking. They had spent infinite hours meandering through the forest paths, climbing trees to sit on branches and watch the birds fly through the skies- their plumage flowing out behind them, graceful and elegant. They would make up poems about the scenery and their feelings.

"Our love was easy. Just being near her made me happy." He explained. "So, one gorgeous evening I decided to ask her to marry me. And she said yes." He smiled wistfully as he said this.

He went silent for a while as he pondered over his memories. I thought of home too. In my youthfulness, I saw only joy in our exile under Chi Sandoz's regime. We moved to a stunning rural area, in the forests Javari was describing. I loved spending days wandering those paths. As a child, I didn't really understand the suffering people were going through. I would see starving families, but we weren't in such a dire situation and I found it hard to empathise. So, whilst there was a rising tension in my home as my parents struggled to adapt to the new ruler, I escaped into the trees.

"She went the colour of death," Javari suddenly explained. "It was just seconds after she agreed to marry me. The warmth of her beautiful, blue cheeks faded to an icy grey."

I listened intently as, for the first time since I had known him, emotion flooded through him. He went on and told me how, before he had realised what was happening, she pushed him. He flew sideways. His head smashed against a pillar at the foot of the driveway where they stood. His memory came to me as a series of fragments that made up these precious seconds. He told me he heard a screech and then she was pinned to the other pillar by an out of control vehicle. It careered straight into her.

All this must have happened in a matter of seconds but the way Javari remembered it, it was as if it was being played in slow motion. He watched the colour drain from her face for hours. The car hurtled towards her for an eternity but he couldn't move to save her.

Her death was instant. There is a saying that death is happy for the person to whom it happens to and a tragedy only to the people left behind. For Javari, he was trapped in a living death from that moment and his life ended. All those beautiful places they had been together, the friends they had shared and the dreams they had were just too traumatic. They were reminders of the life they would never now share. So he left. He vowed never to talk of her because he thought it was the only way to move on. He joined the Army, signed onto Abram's mission, kept his head down and worked hard.

His experiences had left him devoid of fear. He was the perfect soldier.

"What about your family?" I asked. "Weren't they there to support you?

"That's a whole other depressing story. Let's save that for another time." He smiled but his eyes were filled with sorrow.

I pitied Javari and couldn't bear for him to suffer any more than he already had. I knew I had to make things right with Abram. I went to find him and when I did, I threw myself at his feet; I begged him to remember how he loved me and how I loved him and I swore to be the woman he wanted me to be- all he had to do was tell me what he wanted and I would do it. I promised to look only at him for the rest of my life if that was what he wanted.

And he forgave me.

"I only got angry because I love you so much. Seeing you flirting with him angered me. I don't want people thinking my wife is a slut." He paused to ensure his words sank in. "I know how gorgeous you are and I'm not naive- every man wants you. I just can't handle that sometimes. I want you to be happy. Just not with Javari- with me" he said.

"Javari doesn't make me happy, Abe, you do. We talk because we're here together, the three of us." I explained. "I don't have to talk to him. But I promise you there's nothing between us. He loves someone else and I love you."

"Then we can move on. We'll never speak of this again."

When he left the room, I cried for my dignity and pride, for Javari, his lost love and for Abram and my love of him. I felt truly wretched but somewhere in the late hours, I must have drifted off to sleep because I awoke with the sunrise, feeling truly empty.

It was clear Abram had come to bed next to me at some point during the night, but he had already left.

There was a tentative knock on the door followed by Javari creeping in slowly. Without saying a word he came across, sat on the bed next to me and pushed my hair away from my face, so tenderly that I realised it was the first time in a very long time that I had been treated with kindness.

He asked me if I was ok and strangely, with him there, I knew I was. Our eyes locked onto each other and I felt something pass between us. We both instinctively leaned forward and in an instant our lips moved swiftly together. They touched affectionately and gently. We were both testing the waters. Then I felt his tongue gently prise my lips apart. My heart was racing and I became acutely aware of every feeling in my body; my ears rushed, the skin pickled on the back of my neck and then fear and guilt came to my heart.

We pulled away simultaneously. I sprang from the bed and fumbled about with straightening my sheets. He stumbled to the door muttering apologies. He left me there, embarrassed and confused as it dawned on me that I actually felt something for him. Then guilt flooded me as I thought of Abram. I had betrayed him.

It was shortly after this that I learnt, the night I had fallen asleep with Abram under the stars, Javari had only left because Abram had begun to brag about me, calling me a trophy to have on his arm and a political alliance due to my family. I felt used. I wondered if he had ever really loved me or whether he was just a very clever and manipulative man.

I had no choice but to carry on as normal. With just the three of us there, I couldn't very well leave Abram. Nor could I have explained to him why I was upset; he would have killed Javari. But every time he kissed me, or held me, or undressed me, I felt sick inside. I sent my mind far away in these moments so that it wouldn't know what my body was doing. Increasingly my head wandered through the forests back home, hand in hand with Javari. We climbed the trees together and watched the birds.

Chapter Five - Relocation

Once we were sure that we were safe in our current location, Abram and the council decided that it was time to start tracking areas where there were slight outputs of energy that appeared biological. Although few and far between, there were small pockets where life seemed to have survived and our next mission was to find these areas and investigate.

Reinforcements were called for and within a matter of days, a small fleet landed. We were given a crew of 50 heavily armed men. Javari told me that irrespective of the situation at the fort, there was a high probability that we would be met with hostility should we make contact with humans elsewhere.

In my mind, it made sense that we might be met with hostility if we were to come towards them carrying weapons; they would assume we were as dangerous as we thought they were. When I put this to Abram he looked at me as if I were a naive child and told me that I would never understand.

Two members of the biomedical team were sent down to earth in the convoy. Siriah, the highest ranking medical officer, was there to supervise a younger officer in implementing a vaccination programme to ensure we were all immunised against viruses that had been found on Earth.

As yet, we had been lucky and maintained our health but there had been discovery of pathogens to which we had no immunity. It had been determined that none of the viruses discovered would be fatal, but that didn't mean they didn't have the power to make us ill. There weren't many though. It seemed impossible for a planet with such a high population to have so few airborne illnesses so we began to speculate as to as to whether they had been demolished along with everything else here. Of those that did remain, our formula for vaccination had worked consistently.

The new arrivals had very little time to acquaint themselves with their new surroundings. As soon as vaccinations were administered and supplies replenished, we had to set off. The men had brought crafts with them that could carry us through the water as our first leg of the journey was to head North- through a short stretch of sea.

We climbed into the vessels in pairs. They were a series of 25 transparent, rubber globules, perfectly sized for two, with seats that encapsulated us. Inside there was a button to start propulsion, a stick to steer, a button to activate the airtight shield and an oxygen supply. The design was very simple but effective. We could travel in convoy or move off individually as required.

Once we were inside and the shields had been activated, we submerged ourselves into the water. The seas were filled with debris. In the time we had been there, people and animals that found themselves plunged into the water had sunk, bloated, risen back to the surface and sunk back down again. Now they lay there, in their watery graves. Their eyes were bulging and their pale skins were beginning to wash away. They lay there mangled amongst shopping trolleys, boats, wood and cars.

It was hard to tell which injuries were a result of natural decay under the water and those the deadly blasts caused. Blistered skin hung from haggard bodies. Scalps were devoid of hair and clothes draped ragged from their torsos. It was nightmarish.

There was a body of what appeared to be a woman, still clutching her son in her arms. How she had managed to cling on to the child was beyond my imagination, but it must have taken a world of love and determination. I couldn't take it anymore. "Let's get some speed!" I told Samson, my travel companion. He didn't seem to be as moved by what he had seen as I was; he was a military man. That image, though, the one of the mother with her small child, haunted me for years to come.

As requested, he increased our propulsion and we began to zip effortlessly through the water. It wasn't long before we reached land. Our globules were deflated and loaded onto a trailer.

Everyone pulled together to secure the equipment and prepare us for travel by land. Abram instructed the men to search for any supplies we could take that might prove useful on our travels. The land this side of the water was as mangled as the other, making it no easy task to rummage through the wreckage. Men groped through mounds of rubble and clambered over ruins. Small teams trekked off into the distance to see if they could find anything further afield.

I stood and watched it all happen. Abram had no task for me other than to sit next to him whilst he awaited people's return. Josiah, as lead engineer, was responsible for commanding this exercise and deciding which materials might be useful to us as we travelled. I could see no reason why Abram would not want us to both help out but he seemed more interested in maintaining appearances.

Apparently the dynamic of our relationship was changing. Abram was powerful enough to keep me with him just because I was his wife. He was Chi here and my job was to fill the position of his Queen. I wondered what this meant for me. I was an officer previously but not of a high rank. What was I now?

I felt useless. I was used to working and pulling my weight and this made me uneasy. I was powerless to do anything about it. So I sat, as Abram played the loyal, doting partner, and smiled away the hour to keep up the pretence. I wondered what the men thought of us though I doubt Abram cared.

Once Josiah came to inform us that everything was completed and Javari confirmed that the security detail was in place, we were on our way again. I felt intensely guilty when I saw Javari. The guilt wasn't the only feeling though. I found myself looking out for him, willing him to look my way and wondering if he felt the same. He never looked.

Then we were back underway again. The men were all marching except for Abram, Samson, Josiah, Javari and I. We were sat on a vehicle which hovered gently above the ground and moved smoothly along with just a gentle humming. It wasn't as luxurious as the vehicles in Holiteria but it used state of the art technology and suited our purpose perfectly. We kept a slow, steady pace to ensure the men marching could keep up with us.

Our intelligence had us heading west. We followed the path of the coast but, with no humans left to drive or walk the paths and plants ripping through the hard-trodden ground, they were hard to follow and we often found ourselves stamping out new routes. Our vehicle could lift to a height of about one metre, making our journey considerably easier than that of the men moving on foot.

They were worn out, hungry and tired. Nonetheless, they never complained; Abram would not have allowed anyone to grumble or criticise. He viewed complaint as weakness and in spite of the many character flaws I had come to find, people respected him and his opinions. They would have marched all night if he had given the order. Thankfully he did not.

We were just an hour into dusk when he halted the convoy at an intact building standing by a roadside in the middle of a barren countryside.

The building was built of grey stone and had a porch with the words 'The Royal Standard' written outside. There was a white signpost with a board hanging from it outside that reiterated this title and bore what I assumed was a coat of arms. Upon heading inside I was shocked that this might be considered to be of a 'royal standard'. We walked into a reasonable sized entrance hall with a bawdy carpet of deep red with a faded gold print.

We took a door off to the right and walked into a large room that was divided by a wooden bar. Behind the bar were neatly labelled bottles hanging upside down, packets of crisps and nuts and a simple looking machine with numbers and buttons all over it. There were hundreds of glasses. This must have been a public house in its day. Now it was dusty and dirty and plants were creeping in through the windows.

Away from the bar there were small tables with chairs around them. There were cups of drink still at the tables, half eaten bowls of peanuts and bars of chocolate. This room had been abandoned in a hurry. What we didn't know was where the people had gone.

"Could they still be here, Javari?" Abram barked.

"We'll do a sweep of the building, sir." He told him. "G troop-come!" he ordered with a confident air of authority. The men followed him and we waited.

He returned looking sickened.

"Well?" Abram asked, either oblivious to his feelings or disregarding them altogether.

"There are people. They're dead." He replied, clearly trying to portray the matter-of-fact attitude that he knew was expected of him. "If you'd like to send in the medics they can confirm. But it's pretty obvious that they died of radiation poisoning. Look a lot like the ones we saw under the water."

"Very well. Send them up- we plan to stay here tonight so if the bodies are in the way, I would suggest you move them somewhere. Perhaps the men can carry them outside. We don't want to be bothered by the smell." Abram was so cool and cold. I wondered what had happened to him to make him this way. "Oh," he added as an afterthought, "make sure you take some samples of them to send back. Maybe a post-mortem or two?"

"Of course, sir. They are in the basement mainly but we can get them moved."

He turned to me, "Wait here. You shouldn't see this."

Whilst resenting being mollycoddled, I was after all an officer here, I was grateful to not have to see the people being removed. I was especially glad to not have to assist in carrying them.

I couldn't help but picture them though. They would have been sat in here, just like me. They had been drinking and talking and sharing anecdotes about their day. I wondered if they had heard an explosion before the radiation bounded through the walls and into their bodies. I wondered how quickly it had been before they had all fled the room scared. Javari had found them in the basement.

I imagined different scenarios. My favourite was one in which someone had taken control. A brave man had stood up and guided the frightened lambs to the basement, promising them safety he knew wasn't there but reassuring them with the promise of it. They had followed him, willingly. In this scenario their pain had been short-lived. Their blood became thinner, they began to bleed and bruise. Pain gripped their abdomens. They began to feel dizzy. Intense headaches raged through their skulls. But they had only a matter of minutes, if that, between their arrival in the basement and their untimely demise.

Another scenario, one that made me sick to my bones, had them suffering much, much longer. They writhed in agony, vomiting profusely. The room filled with the stench of excrement. In this scenario, brave men killed their own wives and children to spare them their suffering. They had to make fast, irrational decisions of whether it was better to put their large hands around their wives' feeble necks and break them fast, or to hit them around the head with something, hard and metallic that they might find down there, in the basement.

The remaining people then suffered an agonising time, comforting each other, or comforting themselves. They died slowly and in pain. They had no understanding of what was happening to their bodies. They were terrified of what was happening and petrified of what might come next. No time to make peace with their maker, their ending would have been filled with violence and despair.

I couldn't think about it a moment longer. I sat, useless once more, on a tall stall at the bar. A tall woman, with thick blonde hair, pulled back into a scruffy knot at the back of her head looked at me. "What will it be, love?" she asked. Her top was low cut and her breasts were full and rounded, right there at my eye level. Her clothes were tight and provocative and there was a flirtatious gleam in her bright, cerulean eyes.

I jumped, startled, and she disappeared into thin air. I wondered if I had been dreaming. Perhaps I had, perhaps I hadn't. In my mind I used this vision to comfort myself. If this was the woman's soul, coming to me from beyond her death, at least she was as she had been in life. At least she didn't remember her horrific end.

Finally, everyone began to pile back into the room. They looked exhausted and jaded. I asked Abram if it would be ok for me to make everyone a drink from behind the bar; he finally granted me his permission after establishing that, in these exceptional conditions, it would not be too belittling for a woman of my stature. I walked behind the bar, just as the woman in my vision had done, pulled up a glass and poured out a drink.

It tasted dubious. I had tried a few foods and drinks native to the planet in the time I had been there but this was new. I found it hard to believe there could be a whole establishment dedicated to these drinks that burnt as they slid down your throat, warming you through to the core in your stomach and killing every taste bud in your mouth. It turned out to be an acquired taste though and after a couple, it flowed more freely.

We were all in surprisingly good spirits; the men were getting a little too high-spirited perhaps. There were a few arguments that broke out of nothing much at all. For some reason, everyone seemed to be in an unusually aggressive mood.

I had been sitting with a drink by myself and one of the soldiers came and sat next to me, striking up some inane conversation. He was slurring his words and swaying slightly. His hand moved towards my thigh and I firmly removed it. It made his way to the same spot again. The last thing I wanted to do was to make a fuss in front of Abram and get this man into trouble.

"Get your hand off me." I told him calmly.

"Don't pretend you don't love it," he garbled.

"She isn't pretending," Abram's voice sliced through him like a knife. His fist, like steel, smashed into his nose. He fell back off the chair. Abram took my hand and I stepped over him passed out on the floor.

The latter part of the night was just a series of images in my mind:

Abram pulling me into a cupboard under the stairs and kissing me with a fervent hunger as my dress slipped down over my shoulder and his hand pulled my skirt up to my thigh.

Abram passed out on my lap as we sat in the bar watching everyone.

Climbing up the stairs to find myself a room with my head feeling fuzzy and the world spinning around me.

Javari as he held my hand and whispered words into my ear.

We ended up, in a stupor, strewn around the building. I had made it to a bed but remained fully dressed, including my shoes. Nobody else was in the room with me and I was quite glad of this. My initial thought upon waking, as I tried hard to recall everything in my mind, was how much I wished I could remember what Javari had said to me. It overshadowed everything else.

I decided it was best to go in search of Abram so we could begin to fathom what had happened. As I stood up, I felt like I had been punched in the head and the stomach. I felt like I was going to vomit. My body felt heavy and as if my limbs didn't quite belong to me. I was confused and frightened so I called out for help. Nobody heard me, or at least they didn't come if they did. I dragged myself out of bed. My mouth felt dry, but the thought of another one of those drinks consumed me with feelings of nausea all over again.

Conspiracy theories ran through my mind. Had we been poisoned? I went downstairs again, through the sleeping masses, and took a sample of the liquid we had been drinking. I took it out to the vehicle and found the testing kits and equipment brought by the biomedical staff. It was ethanol based. I realised with dismay that we had been drinking alcohol. Any sort of mind altering substance is strictly forbidden in our culture. We pride ourselves on being able to keep a clear mind. I had read about pubs and alcohol. We used ethanol on Holiteria as a fuel and a solvent, but I never thought I would have found myself drinking it.

I went and found Abram next and explained what had happened. He called an immediate meeting of everyone and forbade us to eat or drink anything else from the house.

He sent two men off in search of uncontaminated water for us to drink and we all ate from our rations that had been brought from the Station. Abram decided that the best way to get over our experience was to walk it out of our systems. This seemed all well and good for him to say, but he wasn't the one that was walking; as before, he was sat in the vehicle with the others and me.

Our journey was punctuated with the sound of men outside vomiting. We sat inside, sleeping and working hard to keep the contents of our stomachs where they should have been. My head was pounding and I felt a deep sympathy for everyone outside. To top it all off, Abram was short with me that day and when he is in a foul mood, everybody knows about it.

I wondered if he blamed me for serving up the drinks in the first place.

Chapter Six – Life Again

As it turned out, I needn't have worried. By the end of that day, Abram's woes were long forgotten. He was so happy that his public displays of affection towards me were embarrassing.

When we set off that morning, the sun was rising. There was a slight mist in the air but the sun shone bright and strong. The glorious azure sky was a blank canvas for it to paint its picture on as its dazzling white rays began to weave lines over it.

There were several beads of dew still settled on some of the shrubs we passed by. To begin with they looked like they had the tiniest of little diamonds, twinkling in the light. As we went further on, wild roses blooming through the hedgerows glowed, and the radiant red of the petals reflected in the droplets made them look like pinpricks of human blood. It is funny how even something wonderful can remind you of death. Somehow it was all around us on that planet, even when we couldn't see it.

As we walked further and further west, it became apparent that many structures had escaped the blasts. The further we travelled, the more buildings remained standing and the less horrific the injuries appeared on the dead.

We wandered through a small village where the buildings appeared to be standing, uniformly, together in rebellion. They looked insolent, if that is possible. All painted in a creamy white, flakes breaking away in their abandonment, they had criss-cross patterns of black wood adorning the fronts of them. They looked bold and interesting; I wished there had been someone there to tell us the history of them. I loved how all buildings had a story and a life to share. There was no longer anyone to tell the story of these ones though. So they maintained their stance of unwelcoming non-compliance and kept a watchful eye on us as we passed through and out the other side.

Something about our journey was making me uneasy but Abram told me that I was just suffering from sleeplessness and an overactive imagination. I supposed that he was right; it wouldn't have been the first time my imagination had run away with itself.

By midday the sun was high in the sky. For the first time since arriving there, just a few months earlier, I began to feel mildly warm. It was a summer in England.

We sat together, fifty-three lonely souls in an empty world on a sandy beach, and ate. The food was uninspiring and I thought back to all the fine delicacies at home. That was a mistake- it simply made me resent the tightly wrapped homogenous rations even more.

The waves were rousing. They gradually pulled themselves further up the beach as we sat there and watched them. They wanted to see who we were and what we were doing there.

Most of the men we travelled with didn't have time to sit and become mesmerised by the view in the way I did. A group of five younger men were talking in hushed tones behind me. I lay down on the warm, brown sand, closed my eyes and pretended to sleep as I listened to them.

I heard them jostle and rib each other. They were teasing one about the fact that he had just left his new wife behind to be sent here; they jibed him about the butler she would be screwing in the long months he was away.

"Is there anything I can be doing for you, madam?" one of them said in a mocking voice.

Then another spoke, clearly supposedly mimicking the young man's new wife, "well, it isn't entirely in your job description, but with Mikea away, there are things that just aren't getting done!"

"Madam?" Came the first voice again.

"Oh, come on. Don't play coy with me. We both know a woman has needs"

"Fuck you!" snarled the voice I could only assume was Mikea's. I opened my eyes to witness him stand up and push past the other men, knocking one of them flat to the ground, to go and sit alone.

He left a hysterical group of men rolling around behind him. They had found a topic that made Mikea bite and I imagined that this was going to be a continued source of comedy.

I felt sorry for him. I yearned to go over to him and comfort him; I wanted to tell him that I knew his wife would be faithful to him whilst he was gone and remind him that he knew this too in his heart. Unfortunately, I knew my talking to him would cause more harm that it would good. Mikea was young and attractive and Abram had a jealous disposition. Mikea was already being put through the paces. I didn't want to make it worse.

In many ways, this made for a very lonely existence. I sat there contemplating how it was possible to be surrounded by so many people and yet be so very alone.

I didn't have to ponder it for long though because after just a short rest we were on our way.

The journey was long and arduous. The men trooping behind us were the elite, but even for them it must have been challenging.

Before I knew it, the day had run its course and the sky was ablaze with oranges and pinks. Clouds glowed in hues of indigo and red. It looked immense but it scattered away at tremendous speed.

The colours dispersed though the sky and faded into darkness as the sun sank lower and lower into the horizon.

As the evening closed in, we found more bodies. The people here had taken much longer to die and their demise seemed to have been recent. The thought of their long endured suffering devastated me but Abram seemed to find joy in it. His mood lifted expectantly.

I kept thinking we would stop soon and let the men rest but we kept pushing on under the watchful gaze of the moon.

"Stop!" an anonymous voice hailed out through the cold air. The steady stomp-stomp of boots ground to a halt and a muffle of excitement babbled through the air.

"Wait here" Abram commanded me.

"The rest of you, let's go!"

The officers scrambled out of the carriage and to action. I sat there in the pitch black and listened. Once again, I was being treated as just another woman and excluded from the action. I hated being left there alone; the silence was frightening and my skin prickled. I felt alert and I strained my ears to listen as intently as possible.

A sickly, retching sound barked out through the darkness. It was the sound of a stomach with nothing left to expel. Although I could identify it, it was a sound unlike anything I had heard before. It chilled me. I wished someone would come and tell me what was happening as I realised the commotion was getting nearer and nearer my carriage.

I wasn't sure at that point whether the men were coming back to me or if something sinister was happening. I felt giddy as adrenalin pumped around my body; I sat there, hardly daring to move. I was still. Torches were getting closer. The retching was getting louder.

The boots were crunching the stones right outside the door. The murmuring of voices was now next to my window. I braced myself for what was about to come.

The door swung open and two men dropped a woman with a mop of matted brown hair at my feet. Her head and body were in the carriage. I couldn't see her face because chestnut stands of hair sprawled in every direction, covering it. She coughed again and rolled herself over onto her side. Her eyes opened. A blood-curdling scream pierced the night air as her eyes met mine and for the first time she realised, we weren't like her. Abram's fist came down on her swiftly and struck her across the head to silence her. She whimpered and went silent. Then I realised it was now me who was screaming.

Javari grabbed me around the shoulders and held me tightly. I fell into him and he pulled me close and buried my face in his chest.

"Get her in properly." Abram ordered.

I heard a scrape along the floor as her limp body was pulled across the carriage.

"Everyone out now," he continued, "and where the hell are the medics? I thought I'd sent someone to fetch them?"

Someone disappeared into the darkness to follow up the order.

There was a brief pause in which I didn't dare to move. I was sat there, disappearing into Javari, whilst Abram sat just a few centimetres away as if I didn't exist. He was too busy to notice me or realise how shaken up I was. That was probably a good thing.

"Medics, sir" a voice broke through and was accompanied by the arrival of two of the medical team.

"About time. Right, everyone set up for the night. We'll camp here."

I looked up at Abram and saw him staring intently at the woman before him. She lay there at our feet, lifeless. He looked up at me.

"We'll sleep over there tonight," he said, pointing to a small house. "Javari, take some men and ensure it's secure. Sweep the street too. If this one's anything to go by then there are potentially some live ones still around here. Take weapons."

Javari left.

I looked down at the woman for the first time since she had landed at my feet. Her skin wasn't burnt and blistered like the ones who had been close to the blasts. Her skin was pale and clammy. She stank of excrement. Her belly was swollen and rounded but not as if she was sick, as if she was carrying life. I couldn't help but stare at it. As I looked, I realised her chest was moving up and down; although it was drawing in under the ribcage and was laboured, it was breath and she was alive.

I was contemplating the possibility of the medics being able to save her and how wonderful that would be when Javari jumped back in, startling me afresh.

"All clear, sir" he said, solemnly.

"Very well, then take Atarah inside and ensure she is comfortable. I'll stay here to brief the medics further and will be in shortly."

I followed Javari to the small home that Abram had suggested. The men were filing into the other homes on the street. I supposed one of them belonged to the woman we were fighting to save so, it seemed wrong that we were all rifling through their things, looting, and sleeping in their beds.

Abram strolled through the door moments later and dismissed Javari. We were alone.

"Let's find the bedroom then, sweetheart" he grinned at me. His smile was cheeky and mischievous and under any other circumstance would probably have been endearing, but sex was the last thing on my mind. Abram was the last man on my mind.

I put on a good show to get it over with quickly and Abram, satisfied and exhausted, fell asleep with his arm wrapped tightly around me.

I just stayed there, eyes fixed on the hideous ceiling lamp, as my mind tried to make sense of everything.

The next morning Abram was up and about early. When I woke up, I rushed downstairs quickly, hoping to find someone who could tell me about the woman. My optimism was squashed as quickly as it rose though; she and her baby had died in the night.

A wave of guilt flooded over me. I hadn't realised at the time but my initial thought when I had seen her, after the shock of course, was one of repulsion. She had stunk and although not maimed outwardly by the radiation as others had been, her appearance was still stomach-churning. The word vile came to mind and I quickly pushed it away again and replaced it with tragic.

I didn't want to become like Abram and the others who all seemed to be immune to the horrors of death and war, but I began to realise that it is possible to become desensitised to it when it is everywhere around you.

I repeated a mantra in my mind, 'Her death was tragic. Her death was tragic. Her death was tragic...'

Chapter Seven – A Moment

As we moved further west, it became apparent that the effects of the explosions were less intense here. Ten of Abram's best men were sent on a covert reconnaissance mission to find the next town.

They left on a resplendent morning. It was early and the sky looked indigo. It was warm, by the standards of this region, and people were generally in good spirits. We had put the hideous things we had seen behind us and rested for a few days on a deserted farm. Javari and his team were the only ones who maintained a state of high alert. After we found the survivor, the threat seemed to hang over us, ever present.

I hadn't had a lot of time to speak to Javari because he had been so busy. I found that I missed him. I had grown accustomed to having him there to talk to back when it had just been the three of us here. I missed the affectionate look in his eyes when he spoke to me. He had once brushed his hand, inadvertently across my knee as we had sat looking out to sea, musing over our solitude on the planet. That was a memory that stirred me every time I thought of it, which seemed to be increasingly often. I doubt he realised how aroused I felt every time he looked at me or touched me.

Yet all of these little things made me miss him and so it came to be that I found myself seeking him out and finding reasons to talk to him.

The afternoon after the team had left to investigate the next village, as I looked out of the little window in my room I noticed him walking out to the barn. Abram was busy holding a meeting with the council at the station via our communication link that had been set up in an old study room. This left me alone and with nothing much to do.

As I wandered outside, men were playing a game using some stones that they had found. They had set up a hoop and appeared to be taking it in turns to throw their own stones through it. Every time a stone passed through its target, the hoop was moved further back. By the time I had arrived the hoop was quite far back. I stood and watched for a moment or two, trying not to look impressed, until a howling cheer arose from the players as someone scored a hoop.

Straw was strewn across the grey, concrete courtyard on which the men played. There were still remnants of animal excrement too from the days when I imagined cows and horses and sheep would run freely through the fields. Even the odd feather remained- a reminder of the wandering chickens and ducks. A tractor was rusting in a side shed, green paint flaking from its surface. An array of metal machinery lined up in a second wooden barn. It looked akin to the old fashioned torture equipment found in museums back on Holiteria. They would have looked immense and menacing in their day but now, with rust gnawing at them and weeds growing around them, they were just a sad and useless reminder of a better time.

It was the barn next to this one that I had seen Javari enter. It was another wooden framed building with low, exposed beams inside. Since all the dead livestock had been disposed of, this barn lay empty and, as far as I could see, there was no reason for anyone to enter it. That was definitely where I had seen him go though and I wanted to see him.

It took a moment for my eyes to adjust to the dark of the barn. A ray streaked in through a slight gap between the roof and the outer wall but rather than providing a great deal of light, it simply picked out the pretty dust particles that danced around the room. I didn't see Javari at first - he had settled himself down in a corner, leaning against a bundle of hay. I moved closer.

"Hey you," I smiled. I noted the way my voice swam through the large empty space.

He turned around, unfazed by my intrusion. "I'd hoped you'd see me" he smiled back, "the past three days I've come in here, just waiting for you to find me."

"Why didn't you ask?"

"How could I?"

"Well..."

"We both know what Abram would do if he knew you were here and if he saw me talking to you. He'd be suspicious... and I didn't know if you wanted to-"

I kissed him.

It was a charming, tender kiss. His lips were soft against mine and we dissolved into the moment. I moved my hand down over his back, gently tracing the contour of his spine, and his hand glided up to my hair and his fingers moved softly through it. I shut my eyes and felt the peacefulness around me. When we could control ourselves no longer, I began to move towards the wall, pulling him with me as I went and the intensity in our kiss became stronger as passion overtook us. Not forceful like with Abram... just full of greatness.

"Oh, I've missed you." He sighed, contentedly. I kissed him harder.

I slipped my hand inside his shirt and felt the warmth of his stomach. He stirred his fingers gently across my side and I felt an involuntary moan leave my lips. We wanted each other.

Footsteps moved outside. We parted and hastily straightened our clothes again.

"Javari? What are you doing in here?" A voice questioned from the door.

"Just came in. Was going to sit down and do some quiet reading," he said, picking up a book on a bale of hay next to him and dropping it nonchalantly back again. "Atarah beat me to it though. Seems she was looking for a quiet spot too!" he lied.

He hadn't come to interrogate us though, and didn't seem to care if we were being caught in a compromising moment or not. "Abram needs you," he stated matter-of-factly. "I've been looking for you all over."

Then, in a moment, they were both gone and I was alone. I sat down, picked up Javari's book and read.

I had been able to read and write in most of Earth's languages since I was very young. My mother had thought it was a wasted talent but I was keen to learn anyway and so enrolled myself on a military training programme for civilians. The basic structure of all of the languages is the same and it wasn't difficult to break the codes and pick them up quickly. Their communication was very basic.

I had only ever used those skills to read facts though, and there I was reading a work of creativity; a story from the imagination of one of the people who had lived here was in my hands and the words were filling my mind. It was a story of witchcraft and war. There was a woman too. I stopped after a powerful speech in which she convinced her husband to commit murder to achieve greatness. She was a wonderfully manipulative woman and held so much power over her husband. I wondered if women on this planet were really like that. I wondered if I would be able to command such control over Abram. I doubted it.

I was sitting there, contemplating a world in which women were more powerful than men or at least equal to them and realising how subservient I now was. I decided to speak to Abram to see if I could resume a data analysis role again. I was good at two things, playing the submissive woman and doing my job. Without my job, any power I had ever had was lost. I needed something to be my own again.

A commotion outside roused me from my thoughts. I got up to investigate, taking the book with me. I was keen to find out more about this 'Lady Macbeth'. I stepped out and was confronted by a crowd of men stood in a ring.

"What's going on?" I asked the man next to me.

"Jomia's collapsed" he mumbled.

"Get Abram- now!" I yelled. I pushed through to the centre of the circle. "Everyone to your rooms. Nobody is to leave until you're told otherwise. Avoid all contact with anyone. Move!" I had never been so assertive. I had wondered before what my position was here now, whether I was an officer, a queen, a subservient wife, and now it didn't matter. Everyone was listening to me and taking my direction. I had never been so dominant in a group of men nor would I ever have dreamed that they would have obeyed. Yet here I was!

My joy was short lived when I looked down. Jomia lay there, curled up, clutching at his stomach. His skin appeared clammy and moist. He reached out to me, writhing in pain, and I backed away. It was unheard of for a Holiterian to get ill.

Josiah ran out first, followed closely by Abram and Javari.

I explained what had happened. Abram sent Josiah to assemble a medical team, while I was sent to get safety masks. Javari set to work arranging a quarantine room in one of the out buildings.

Until we knew what we were dealing with it was essential to be cautious. In an alien world full of unknown pathogens which our bodies were not equipped to deal with, any virus not caught in time could prove fatal. Jomia was a strong man and if it had taken him down, it seemed likely that it could kill any of us!

I returned with the masks and soon after the medics arrived in containment suits.

They wore shiny silver suits from head to toe and moved slowly because of the bulky protection that surrounded them. The scene was reminiscent of images we had seen of the first time a human went to their moon. The 'spacesuit' was hilarious in its primitiveness yet there was nothing funny to be found about the scene unfolding before us.

What happened next was a series of hushed conversations and meetings behind locked doors. Later that evening Abram confessed to me that our vaccination system was ineffective against the strain of virus Jomia was fighting. Our bodies were defenceless and he was being annihilated from within. The fact that he even thought to tell me this showed me just how worried he was.

As darkness fell, he spent hours typing notes into his handheld, pacing around our room like a caged animal. I tried to sleep but felt restless. So I sat up, hugging my knees and watching him.

Clearly I looked frightened, which given the scenario we were in was only natural. Abram, in a moment's kindness, saw that in me and comforted me in the only way he knew how: he made love to me.

Afterwards, he held me tightly and told me that everything would be all right. He said that he had the best men working on fixing our problem, so I had no reason to be concerned. I wasn't sure if he was trying to reassure me or convince himself. Either way he was right. We were lying still, both pretending to be asleep, when there was a knock at the door.

It was Siriah, the chief medical officer, "Sir, sorry to interrupt you but this is important. We were right about the antibodies in the placenta. We have used them-"

"Not here" Abram hissed, "details later."

Siriah glanced quickly at me, dropped his gaze and apologised. Clearly there were some things I wasn't supposed to know. The conversation went on but became stilted, with minimal details, as Siriah grappled with what he might or might not say in front of me.

"Is Jomia alright?" Abram asked.

"Yes, sir. A treatment was devised"

"And a vaccine?"

"Here, sir."

"Super. Let's administer now. How many do you have?"

"Plenty for now, sir. The problem is these are unknown antibodies. We've no idea how long they'll last. Our bodies might break them down, in which case, they will need to be administered again. That's the problem with passive immunity. We'll need to keep running checks."

"Administer six. Atarah and I first. Then Jovari, Josiah and yourself. Save the last. Malachi will join us soon and it makes sense he has one too."

"Very well, sir. Atarah, do you mind if I-" he held up the needle and gave me a nod.

"Go ahead," I agreed. I wasn't entirely sure what was happening but I was sure a refusal wasn't an option.

He walked over to me and, in the silvery glow of the moonlight, he injected me in my arm. Once Abram and I had both been administered our shots, he left as quickly as he came.

"What was that all about?" I asked.

"We have a vaccine and were able to treat Jomia. Don't worry about the rest, sweetheart, it all worked out well." He said breezily.

"But how? What about the others?"

"Shhh." He touched my lips. "You know how much I hate discussing work with you..." His words trailed off as he leaned over to remove the sheets from around me and looked lustfully at my body.

This time it wasn't about comforting me or forgetting about his own fears; he was confident again and feeling powerful.

Chapter Eight - Phase One

That morning the men were brought out of their quarantine. There was a hum of interest around Jomia and his miraculous recovery. Jomia had been unaware of everything that had been happening around him while he was ill and couldn't give everyone the answers they were looking for. Abram quickly called a meeting for everyone to attend. The first order of business was to praise the medical staff and make it very clear that nobody was to ask questions yet. All information was to be released as and when it was necessary to know. It seemed like those answers were going to remain unobtainable.

The rising tide of secrecy disturbed me.

The second order of business was Abram's big announcement. In his communications with the station and back home, the future of this planet had been discussed in great lengths. It had been decided that Abram should officially take position here as Chi. He had, after all, been masquerading in the position since everyone arrived anyway.

He had arranged for many more men to be dispatched here- men that were prepared to settle here- and women were coming too. Men were having their wives relocated to be with them, children in tow where children existed. A selection of single women would arrive too. Life from Holiteria was arriving in order to continue business.

And as for the business? Well, we were to build large hospitals. The humans that remained were weakened and ill. Abram explained that we would set up hospitals and administer the aid they needed. He described it as a charitable gesture to the people here.

Everyone had listened in silence. After Abram departed, he left behind a confused mass of people, with a cloak of mystery surrounding them. The men shuffled and whispered amongst themselves, excited at the prospect of seeing their loved ones again. I am sure it was a shock to discover that their entire lives, including their families, were being relocated to Earth. They hadn't been consulted. They knew, however, that their job involved respecting their orders.

They had very little time to prepare for these changes. That afternoon the first crafts arrived.

The transportation was much larger than the small silver ship we had arrived in. I always wondered why in Earth's understanding of extraterrestrial life we travelled around in flying saucers. In reality our engineers converged on a shape and design much more similar to their own rockets. I imagined that they would be disappointed on discovering the truth. The main difference was the propulsion system. A chemical reaction between two heavy transuranic elements, discovered in laboratories by scientists on Holiteria, were reactive enough to produce the kinaesthetic energy required to propel us swiftly up out of the Earth's or our own planet's atmosphere and plunge us into the depths of space. Our technological advancements meant that we were able to exert much greater control over our vessels on re-entry into another planet and could explore for much longer without the need to refuel.

The wave of passenger crafts came to earth, controlled and stately. When the doors lifted open and family members streamed out, the control disappeared and was replaced with wild jubilation from the crowds waiting to greet them.

It was so pleasing to see the families reunited; everyone deserved it. Men, women and children were hugging each other so tightly they looked like they might shatter. Young lovers came together with romantic embraces and passionate kisses. The single men stood on one side of the gathering and looked longingly at the single women, who stood nervously on the other side.

They had their travel hats on and clasped their bags nervously to their sides. Bewilderment filled their faces and I wondered what promises they had been brought here with. They were all stunning; somebody had clearly had orders to select the finest women Holiteria had on offer. Standing there, a sea of gorgeous silver curls and lips painted bright blue, their faces filled with tears as they watched the happy families around them and it dawned on them what they had left behind.

I walked over to Abram. "Is there anything I can do to settle these women in? They look petrified."

"Don't worry," he reassured me, "I have a plan." He gave me a knowing wink and with that, he addressed the men that did not have partners and instructed them each to choose themselves a woman.

Although I knew that it was forced love and the women had practically been brought here to act as glorified prostitutes, I couldn't help feeling a pang of emotion when I saw them together. There was something about seeing a couple together when they have a whole new relationship, full of potential love and promise, laid out before them. It made me think of Javari.

With a sudden horror filling my heart, I wondered if there was a woman here that was earmarked for Javari. After all, Abram was hardly likely to leave his most trusted security advisor with nobody, even if they did have their differences on a personal level. My eyes desperately surveyed the crowds to find him.

I began to twist through the gathering, searching for him. The jovial chattering sounded distant and empty and the flashes of laughing faces swum mockingly in front of me. I was becoming consumed by hideous jealousy.

Just as I thought I might faint, a pair of hands appeared around my waist and turned me gently around. An enormous smile overtook my face as I spun around and found myself confronted with...Abram.

Disappointment filled my heart. He looked so pleased. His loyal subjects were here now and he could take his position as Chi. "Come with me," he said as he placed his hand on the small of my back and beckoned me to move forward.

"I was just-" I began.

"Whatever it is can wait. We need to be seen together, united." He retorted.

I wondered how Javari felt when he saw us together. Did he feel as sick to his stomach thinking about it as I did when I had to imagine that he might be with another woman?

Abram walked me up to a raised platform that had been erected. Unlike the hastily crafted podium of his first rally, this was beautiful. On it sat two ornately crafted thrones.

"I had these commissioned for us as a present to you," he beamed.

"They're gorgeous!" I gushed. I was honestly impressed.

"Then sit on that one and look beautiful," he suggested, pointing, "Whilst I speak."

He stood up and silence fell before him. His ability to do that never failed to astound me. He began:

"Firstly, let me welcome you. This is a planet of abundance and joy and I know you will not regret your decision to come here. We are in an exciting time of promise..."

My mind began to wander as I cast my eyes out over the crowd.

I watched one of the women, who had arrived as a gift, in the arms of Jomia. I knew she wasn't a partner from home. We'd had a brief conversation in the past where he mentioned how he missed his bachelor lifestyle back home. She was brazen and lustful and was dressed in stark contrast to the plain clothes they were wearing upon arrival. It occurred to me that she was now putting on an act, and they had perhaps known that they were being brought here to be sold. As it turned out, I was right - they did.

Five more crafts arrived over the course of the afternoon filled with strong, brave looking men who had agreed to move with their families for the promise of a better life on Earth. Abram and I sat there on our thrones for what seemed like hours whilst they came to nod their respects at us and touch my hair. This custom tired me. I wondered how long-standing wives of Chis put up with it!

I had obviously been temporarily lost within my mind because whilst I had been contemplating this, Javari had slid silently and unnoticed onto the stage next to us.

"Sir," he began, "a call from the Government of the People awaits you in the comms room."

"Thank you. You can stand there and keep Atarah company whilst I'm gone." He ordered.

I felt all the blood running to my cheeks.

All I wanted to do was ask him who was here for him, ask him if he had chosen a woman to be with. The words stuck in my throat and I didn't know how to say them. My mouth went dry and my mind raced. As much as I wanted to know the answer, I was afraid of what it might be.

"My sister's here," he smiled warmly, "with her husband and their two little boys. It's so lovely to see them." He gazed into my face as if he was reading my mind. "There are enough women here for me to have one too, if I wanted one."

"And do you?" I whispered.

"There is one I want," He grinned.

"Oh," I said, unable to mask my sadness.

"Atarah, it's you. You make me feel things I never thought I'd feel again after... after everything" he said gently and quietly. He might have been feeling new things again but he still choked on Marelli's name.

I tried to contain the smile. I didn't want to sit there grinning like an idiot on this stage in front of all these people.

"We need to find a time to talk properly," I told him, "I want you too. More than I have ever wanted anyone else before! I wish I could see a way it was possible," my voice trailed off as Abram returned.

"Thank you, Javari. I have it from here. Go have some fun with one of those young women" he winked.

Javari walked away and Abram took his place beside me again.

It filled my heart with joy to know that, even if he was with someone else, I was the one that held Javari's heart.

Abram finally announced it was time for everyone to go home. Three of his officers were assigned the duty of overseeing this and making sure everyone was given a residence in the nearby town. Abram and I would continue to stay here on the farm, along with a few of his most trusted men. My heart leapt for joy when I realised one of those men was Javari. I prayed that we would find an opportunity to get together.

There was no time for them to settle into the way of life here. Everyone was given one night together uninterrupted but the next day the men were to report to a secret location and set to work on building the first giant hospital complex.

They began by erecting an elaborate array of sprinklers. They rose, tall and shiny from the ground and stood six feet above my head. They looked scary and intimidating. Abram explained to me that they were spraying something over the soil that would enable them to remove the caesium-137, a radioactive isotope that was released during the explosions. It is severely damaging to the humans. They had to cleanse the area before they began or it would be an unsuitable location to house any of them.

Some isotopes of caesium have a half life of up to 30 years and the way it bonds with the soil after a nuclear explosion has always caused scientists on Earth difficulties about how to remove it. They had experimented, with some success, the use of Prussian blue nanoparticles and acidic solutions. Holiterian scientists had refined the vitrification process and could stabilise radioactive waste from vast areas in an incredibly short space of time. I don't pretend to know the science behind the process; it looked simple enough when the vast machines were spraying the solution over the soil but I imagine the knowledge that went into it was incredible as our greatest scientists had been working on it.

Once the grounds were cleared, they worked tirelessly to build the establishment using plans drawn up by a Holiterian architect under Abram's direction. The building was immense in size and elaborate in design.

I watched it grow upwards, stone by stone. I didn't get the chance to go there often. For a start, I didn't want to get in the way. They were working tirelessly to get it built and came home late into the night every day to return to their wives, exhausted. Then, it would start all over again as the sun rose the next morning.

They worked with boundless loyalty, determination and motivation. They believed in our cause unquestioningly because Abram had told us that we were doing the right thing. Not one man or woman, having seen the immeasurable improvement he had made to their homes in Holiteria, would have thought him capable of anything other than working for our greater good. He was honourable, just and always right in our eyes at that time.

Each time I went to visit, the building was a stage taller, until finally, it was completed. I felt proud of what we were doing for this planet. We were offering its inhabitants a chance to recover. I genuinely believed we were doing a wonderful thing.

At some point during the process of building the hospital, the men who had gone off to search for nearby survivors returned.

They had been gone a long time and I realised as they came back that we should have been worried about this, but there had been so much happening here that we were too busy to notice. Perhaps Abram was aware of their absence but he had not mentioned it to anyone if he was.

They too had family there waiting for them. I suppose they must have missed them and worried. There are small fragments of the puzzle, like this one, that I cannot quite piece together. Abram's secrets were vast. He kept his darkest plans closest to his heart and shared them with no one.

Their mission had been a success though.

They had almost reached the west coastline before they reached what they were looking for; a town with survivors.

They described a small town by the water's edge. Golden sands stretched out towards crystal clear water. There were huge white birds with pale grey wings; they had yellow beaks that had the tiniest splodge of red on their tips. In the absence of humans, these birds seemed to rule the beaches.

Standing to attention on the dilapidated walls that separated the sand from the tarmac, they called out loudly asserting their position. Unperturbed by the presence of these strangers, the birds were cocky and had no qualms with stealing food from them. Back at home it was unheard of for a creature to have such confidence but here it seemed it was normal.

These scavengers quickly became pesky but they did serve as a useful alarm clock as they made their noisy morning debuts each day.

Not long after finding these birds, other life began to materialise. A shoal of fish splashed just beneath the surface of the sea much to the excitement of a flurry of the grey birds. Later, a rat was seen scurrying through a building. Insects began to appear- thick webs began to grow across doors, with spiders housed securely in the centre. The more life they found, the more cautious they became.

Finally, under the cover of darkness, they stumbled across human life. The people were sickly, but not dying. They crept amongst their homes once everyone was asleep and completed a silent census. They saw the looted shops, with windows shattered and doors smashed in. The humans had completed the destruction the explosions began.

These stories excited me. I retold them to the other women as if I had been there myself. I have probably elaborated on them over time, but it was the first real acknowledgement of life we discovered on the planet after our arrival. I was excited and full of hope.

The human survivors seemed, in the main, desperate and forlorn. Most had little energy in their unhealthy state and appeared despondent. The army had expressed that it was saddening to see.

The soldiers returned with completed reports and presentations to give. They imparted their knowledge with as much precision and detail as they possibly could because they knew that mistakes might threaten our entire mission. We were often reminded of the delicacy of our situation.

By the time the site of our hospital had been completed, we were late into autumn. During this time, more intelligence had been gathered and analysed and we were ready for the next phase begin.

Chapter Nine- Phase Two

The day that phase two began was accompanied by snow. Soft white flakes fell from the sky over the course of the evening and by the morning there was a thick, cold heap smothering the ground. It was the strangest thing we had ever seen. To begin with we were cautious. Initially we had assumed it was some sort of blossom. When we realised it wasn't, alarm bells began to ring. It took longer than I would care to admit for us to realise that it was the snow we had read about and seen photos of.

Children viewed it with excitement, throwing it, rolling in it and kicking it. Then the adults started to follow and before we knew it, everyone was out in the fields together, playing and having fun. Babies were wrapped in layer upon layer of golden fur. Thick fluffy coats, hats, shawls, socks and boots were all brought out to ensure that the bitter cold did not ruin the fun.

Inside, fires were crackling. This was where Javari and I found some time to be alone: by the heat of a fire, on a thick deerskin blanket. In the exhilarating pleasure found in the arrival of snow, we had been able to slip away unnoticed.

We lay there, the light from the fire flickering over our half naked bodies, my head propped up on his chest whilst he gently ran his fingers through my hair.

"It's killing me being apart from you," he confessed.

"Me too," I told him. "I keep fantasising, trying to think of ways we can be together."

"I know... me too," he looked at me with sadness in his eyes, "I never thought I could love like this again. It was too painful before.

But I fell for you long before I realised it had happened. It just seems so unfair that even now, I can't have my happiness."

I reached up and kissed him again. I pulled back, looked deep into his eyes and removed my lip ring.

That gesture said more than any words could have. In that single, unspoken moment, our relationship solidified itself and our hearts truly belonged to each other.

He rolled me over, rose onto his elbows and we made love.

Afterwards, we spent a long time talking. We discussed our dreams and desires. We spoke of life here. During a natural lull in the conversation, I decided it was the right time to ask him something I had wondered for a long time. "What's the story with your family?" I asked. He visibly tensed. "I'm sorry. Obviously you don't have to tell me."

"No, it's fine, honey. I want you to know everything about me. It's just that it was a tough thing for me to come to terms with."

"Well we don't have to talk about it now. Whenever you're ready."

"I am ready." He took a deep breath. " I lost my parents when I was six."

"Oh! I'm so sorry. I didn't realise." I didn't know what to say.

"I watched them die at the hands of criminals. Bastards looking to steal what they could from our home. My mum hid with me in the cupboard and my father confronted them. He was a proud man. We both saw him die."

"How awful." I gently pushed my hands through his hair and looked at the pain in his eyes.

"And I gasped. I couldn't help it. My mother wanted to protect me so she pushed me deeper under a pile of coats and they pulled her out. They pulled her out and I heard her die. She died because of me." Tears formed in his eyes. He blamed himself for his mother's death and had lived with that guilt and pain since the age of six. There was nothing I could say. I held him tightly and we stayed there together in silence.

I couldn't tell you how long we were there, but as the sun rose high into the midday sky we knew it was time to go our separate ways.

Putting my lip ring back in and returning to Abram was so painful. I wanted to stay and comfort Javari. I wanted to take away all the pain he had suffered in his life. I wished I could have seen a way for things to work in our favour. Knowing an end to my life with Abram was possible would have made it so much easier to continue the charade... but Abram was Chi. We were already taking a huge risk to spend time together. If he knew about our relationship, he could have us exiled or killed, or punished in whatever way he saw fit. Our love was treason.

Luckily I returned before I was missed. I arrived just in time to join everyone for lunch and I laughed alongside the stories of slipping, snowballs and fun as if I had been there. I buried Javari's pain deep inside. Abram too was in high spirits because of the morning's rest. It was the first day without work since the latest recruits had been brought here. With the hospital finished, it was a welcome break from manual labour.

And with the hospital finished, Abram decided that it was a good time to explain what was going to happen next.

The intelligence collected from the Station had estimated that there were currently no more than 105,000 people alive on Earth. 10,000 people in total were in England, where we currently resided. The estimated number was dropping as every day passed, without anything to treat the radiation poisoning. It had been estimated that of the 105,000 people alive, by the end of three months without help from our teams, only 20,000 would remain. So we had to act fast.

The task was to round up every single person we were able to find and return them to the hospital- regardless of their health condition. Though we did not have beds or rooms for all of the individuals, the hospital was large and they would easily crowd into rooms with mattresses on the floor. Comfort was a luxury. At this stage, we were solely focused on giving them life.

That afternoon, in the cold, thick snow, troops set off in different directions with the equipment needed to track potentially human sources of energy. Abram waited here to act as commander-in-chief of the hospital as patients were brought in.

Whilst they were gone, a second site had been located and further men had been tasked with building a second hospital. The plan was to fill this one with patients brought from the rest of the globe. Ultimately, Abram saw all living humans, safely locked up in a series of hospitals, right there in England, where we treat them and return them to health.

As Chi, it seemed he viewed himself as leader of both races: us and them.

The winter passed slowly and the snow grew tiresome. Despite this, the new hospital developed rapidly and everyone was pleased with the results, especially as once it was completed they no longer had to work outside in the biting winds and icy frosts.

And the patients began to arrive, slowly at first, then in a steady stream until our first building was full. We continued to cram them in. Rooms were filled with twenty people in conditions ranging from nearly dead, to weak but non-critical. Once we were sure that we could fit no more people in, the second hospital was opened.

Then followed a third, and then a fourth. Each hospital site was cleared of radiation using our technology to ensure that our patients would survive and thrive in their new settings.

In those four locations across England we cared for 30,607 patients from across the globe. We were confident there was nobody else out there alive, and the medics began the treatment programme. The number of survivors was a lot lower than initial figures had suggested but I supposed we should have been grateful for that. We couldn't have fitted many more in.

The pride of our endeavours was felt across our whole community. The women would talk about it animatedly during mornings spent together whilst the men worked. They discussed the heroic deeds of their husbands, who it seemed were so modest that they didn't feel the need to talk about it, with any of them. They complained about how hard their husbands had to worked. It was understood that this was the hardest phase though, as it was essential to bring the humans back to full health. Once they had recovered, the women were sure it would get better.

The men were clearly finding the strain taking a toll on them too. I had noted with some interest that many men seemed to be turning to drinking the forbidden alcohols in the evenings when they returned from work. The women were becoming increasingly frustrated. They felt like their loved ones were shutting them out. I realised it had been a long time since I had spoken to Javari too. I needed to find him and see how he was.

Before I had a chance to do that, a letter arrived for me. Someone wearing a hat pulled down low over his face thrust it into my hand; he was discreet and quick and it was clear this letter was unofficial.

I stuffed it into my top and rushed home. Abram was there waiting.

"Good day?" he asked.

"Not too bad," I told him. "Just been for lunch with some of the officers' wives. They think you're working their husbands too hard."

"Oh?"

"Yes, their husbands hardly have time to speak to them!"

"Well I will be sure to ease up on them" he said. His voiced sounded strangely smug. I hoped I hadn't talked out of turn. He pondered for a moment. All I could think about was the letter nestled close to my chest; my hand reached instinctively to the place where it sat under my top. I prayed it was from Javari.

Eventually, he spoke, "Well, your husband isn't lacking in time for you."

"That's true," I mused, slightly confused by our conversation.

"In fact," he continued, "What do you think of producing an heir."

His words fell heavily at me, choking me as if he had put his hands around my neck and squeezed. I knew this question was like any other order he gave. I mustered a smile and thought of Javari.

"Well?" he demanded.

"That sounds wonderful!" I gushed, hoping I sounded sincere. "I'm sorry, it was just a surprise. A lovely surprise!"

"Excellent," he declared proudly, "I will make arrangements for the doctor to come tomorrow and reverse your API. Maybe tonight we can have some fun practising."

The API was an Anti-Pregnancy-Immunisation. Every girl is administered one at puberty and has it reversed when you and your husband apply to the doctor.

I smiled as broadly as I could. "This is so exciting. It's about time we got some practise in- you have been far too busy lately." I told him, knowing that was exactly what I was expected to say.

My mind was in overdrive: how would I make this work with my relationship with Javari? Was he suggesting this because he knew I was being unfaithful? Why now?

"I think it will be lovely that our son will be the first child born in this new home!" He went on, clearly stepping back from husband and into the political role.

"Or daughter," I added coyly, keeping up the pretence of my joy.

"Of course," He replied, but his mind was already elsewhere. "Let me contact the doctor."

With that, he left the room.

I rushed upstairs and threw myself on my bed, clutching at the covers. Then I remembered Javari's letter, pulled it from its hiding place and tore it open expectantly. But it wasn't from him.

In gorgeous cursive manuscript, it declared:

Dearest Atarah,

It is with regret we must write this letter to you and we trust it reaches you safely. Amongst the leaders here there are serious concerns as to Abram's motives. They began to suspect him when he proclaimed himself the Chi after abolishing the power it carried here. He had the Government of the People tell the citizens on Holiteria it was their suggestion that he be given that title. It is with worry that we must confirm this is not the case. Your father overheard a conversation in which it was made very clear the Government of the People do only as they are told by Abram.

The people here say he is secretive and his motives are unclear. The Government of the People tell us they are unable to react to him.

They tell us it is because there is no proof that he is acting in an untoward way. There has been a suggestion that he is holding something over them.

I would ask you to keep your eyes open and be vigilant. I sincerely hope that our worries are misguided... in case there is some truth here, stay safe, my dear.

All our love,

Your devoted parents.

I was confused. Abram wasn't without his flaws but he had done a lot of good here. If it weren't for him, humans would be extinct by now. They seemed more susceptible to the radiation than any of the plants or other animals native to the planet.

I knew what I needed to do. I went in search of Javari. He was the one person that I knew could be trusted to protect my parents and who would tell me the truth. I secretly wanted a reason to be able to talk to him too. I hadn't seen him in weeks and I missed him sorely. I didn't manage to find him though. Abram had sent him to one of the other hospital sites for a month; this explained his absence from my life. Luckily he was due back soon.

Miraculously, by the end of that week, the women were reporting that their husbands were much more conversational in the evenings and were singing the praises of the hospitals. I felt like at least one good thing had come out of this horrible situation; it had put Abram in a good mood and the men were reaping the benefits. I have to say that this set my mind at ease somewhat.

I was also relieved that Abram had to travel to hospital 3 to deal with a problem that had arisen. One of his men had been hurt in an accident and it sounded serious. They weren't sure if he was going to make it.

Although my API was reversed, I didn't need to worry about pregnancy until he was back. I hoped Javari would come back before him.

Chapter Ten – The Truth

As it turned out, luck was on my side. Javari returned first. He had been driving in a flashy red car that had been found here on Earth. The engineers had taken some of the best cars they had found and modified their engines to make use of the technological advances we had on our planet. We didn't want to drive around in vehicles that used the polluting engines that humans had used.

Once I was sure it was him that I had seen returning, I called downstairs to where I knew Josiah was sitting.

"Josiah! Quick!" I shrieked.

He came running up the stairs as quickly as he could.

"I...I think I saw someone looking in the window!"

"One of us? Or human?" He asked.

"I er.. I really couldn't be sure..." I lied. "Maybe I imagined it... I don't feel right with Abram away.' I made my eyes fill with tears.

"How about I send Javari up to check everything out?" he asked, desperate to get away from an emotional woman.

It had worked as I had planned. "Please... that would be a great help... I would feel much safer."

I felt a little guilty because Javari rushed over, panicking, thinking there was truth in my story. "I didn't see anyone." I informed him. "I'm sorry. I just really needed to see you. Please don't be mad."

He gently kissed the tears away from my eyes and I realised they were now real. "How could I ever be mad with you," he said warmly, "especially for just wanting to see me. I've missed you so much, it drives me crazy."

The words tumbled out of my mouth. I told him about my letter, then the baby, not giving him time to respond in between either. I was worried that if I didn't get all the information across quickly then I wouldn't be able to say it at all. When I had finished, I collapsed in a heap on the bed and lay my head gently on his lap.

Time stood still for us as he sat there, unsure what to say.

When he began to speak it was clear he was struggling to find the right words.

"There's no easy way to tell you this, but there is a reason the men have started talking to their wives more," he began. "Unfortunately, our work load hasn't changed and neither has what we are doing, but we have been given specific orders to ensure everyone here and everyone back home knows how wonderful the hospitals are."

He went on to tell me what was really happening at the hospitals. For a start, the accident that Abram had gone to investigate was no accident at all. It was a message to all of them; the man was dead and it was no accident. He had refused to carry out a direct order and so Abram had been contacted. Abram had ordered his execution. Everyone inside the hospitals knew it. Their families were not to be told. They were all living a double life. Abram was bribing them with nice houses, luxurious foods and was in the process of setting up a monetary system to reward them financially too.

The money would help their wives set up shops in our village and the hope was that we could begin to generate an economy. This had led to a real buzz in the village and the men didn't want to take away the hope from their families.

I asked why he had refused to follow out an order. Then the horror of what was happening was unravelled. The hospitals were more like prisons, with cramped and dirty conditions. Those that were too sick or deformed or that might not be useful in the future were euthanized. The reason the numbers of patients was so much lower than we had initially thought was because anyone terminally ill or above the age of 60 had been killed.

I couldn't believe the implication of what he was telling me. The letter suddenly felt real. It occurred to me for the first time that the fears people had might be a reality. I couldn't imagine any reason why Abram would be treating these people in such appalling ways and it sickened me.

Javari was reluctant to tell me any more; he shouldn't have even told me that. I knew that there was only one way for me to find out what was really going on. My mind started to process what I had been told.

"And as for the baby," his words infiltrated my thoughts and pulled me back, "I love you and I know what you have to do. I'll love you and your child." He looked like he was going to say something else but checked himself.

"Go on..."

"That was all. I will love you both."

He looked sheepish. "You aren't being entirely honest with me." I stated. I was worried.

"I was going to suggest something, but it's wrong, maybe too wrong."

I had to wrangle the idea out of him. But finally he said it:

"What if you have my baby?"

My mind was swimming. The hospitals, the baby. Javari felt horrible for suggesting it. But he needn't have done. While it was true that we hadn't been seeing each other romantically for very long, the one thing I was clear about more than anything else was how I felt about him. It felt like a good idea. If I ever found a way to leave Abram, then Javari and I could be together and the child I had would be our own. I was so overwhelmed with the roads unravelling before me that the downsides didn't cross my mind. Javari's offer was exactly what we both needed; a baby together gave us a rock to cling to in the rough seas of uncertainty around us.

I am sure neither of us had time to think it through logically but it didn't matter. We went with our hearts and the thought of having Javari's child made me feel the anticipation and pleasure that I should have felt when my husband suggested it.

The excitement of knowing we were doing something illicit gave me a heady feeling. I wanted to savour every single moment of it and I wanted to feel everything. The smell of clocoli flowers filled the room. It was insane to believe it but it was true. The fragrant scent that had filled the air the first time I felt Javari touch me had returned and was blessing us as we made love.

Our race isn't prone to the difficulties of conception, nor are we tied to a monthly cycle of timings the way humans are. By the end of that afternoon, I knew I was pregnant.

When Abram returned home two days later, I made sure that sleeping together was the first thing we did. He was pleased at my eagerness and misread it as excitement on my part. It wasn't until afterwards that I began to feel guilt. I had tricked Abram and robbed him of his opportunity to have a child and heir of his own. In an effort to justify this to myself, I thought of the horrific things I had heard about the hospitals. In my mind I painted him as the vilest of monsters; I needed to believe that he deserved what he got. He was Chi Sandoz when he claimed to be Chi Mayniah.

The world felt like it was crushing me. I had acted hastily and now I realised the gravity of my actions and their implications. If Abram and I somehow separated, he would be furious to learn that his child wasn't his. I couldn't imagine he would willingly let Javari and I be together knowing we had been together behind his back. As long as he was Chi, Javari and I had to be apart. I was plunged into darkness. My chest felt tight and I was breathing much quicker than I should.

I had to distract myself from this situation. I had to hope and believe that things would work themselves out. I decided to throw myself into another pursuit; I needed to know the truth about the hospitals.

Chapter Eleven – A Mission of Discovery

I couldn't very well have asked Abram if I would be able to go and visit a hospital. He clearly would have refused, as he was going to extreme lengths to hide the truth from anyone who didn't need to know, including me. Besides, if I had asked him and he had said 'no' I couldn't have feigned ignorance if he caught me there.

I had to wait for the perfect time, which as it turned out, was about a month away. The relentless cold of winter was beginning to subside and there were even the odd areas of green vegetation poking through. Rains were falling regularly and the grounds were heavily laden with thick mud. The villagers were happy, feeling the encroaching warmth of spring.

Women were enjoying working in the shops they were running. An older lady, called Blayrei, had set up a small clothing boutique. Although her youth had long since passed her, she had a fabulous sense of style and with the help of her husband, Malachi, had been able to set up a communications link to home to enable her to keep up-to-date with the latest fashions. She had instructed two of the younger women in the art of tailoring, and with her designs and their newly founded skill, business was blooming. I knew Shallimi, the lady who had designed my wedding dress, would be joining us soon and I recommended her to join the venture as well.

Women were wearing black visors over their faces, huge furry capes, smooth tailored black jumpsuits and boots that reached up to their thighs with pointed heels and rounded toes. The men certainly seemed to appreciate their efforts too.

Josiah's wife had set up a supermarket. We had a bakery, a restaurant and bank. Spring was coming, the villages were running like clockwork and the men appeared to be happy; at least superficially, our new society was running smoothly.

It seemed like a perfect time to visit a hospital. Nobody would question my motives because I was pregnant, happy, contented... what reason had I to doubt anything?

I set off not long after Abram left to visit hospital two. I decided to visit hospital one. It was the closest to my residence and furthest from hospital two.

When I arrived, two guards stood at the entrance greeted me. The building looked drab and melancholy. Tall wire fences ran around the perimeter of the grounds. On top of it was a mangled twist of wires that stared down with sharp, menacing eyes. People trudging through the oozy mud had formed paths just inside the fences. Everything before me was a blur of greys and browns. It certainly didn't look like the cheerful, hopeful place I had envisioned.

"Can I help you, Ma'am?"

"Yes, Abram sent me. I'm here to check your inventories." I lied with grace and poise. The two guards looked at each other uneasily. One shrugged and the other relaxed slightly. They nodded in the direction of the front door and stepped aside.

I wish there were words to describe to you the stench that burnt my nostrils as I walked in. It was the smell of death and decay.

Although the unpleasant odour lingered with me, the entrance hall was quite grand. There was a lot of white and it had a clinical feel as you would expect from a hospital, but the receptionist's desk was formed of a thick, dark piece of wood, elegantly carved. An ornate coffee table sat in the centre of the room with sofas surrounding it.

Everything about the room was suggestive of wealth and stirred confidence in the aims of the hospital. I imagined humans arriving there hurt and frightened, but those feelings dissipating slightly and being replaced by relief when they realised how well looked after they would be here.

I began to wonder about what Javari had told me.

"Can I help you, Ma'am?" asked the man behind the desk.

"Yes, Abram has sent me. I'm Atarah. I'm here to check inventory lists."

"Yes, Ma'am, I know who you are. I'm just surprised. Abram said nothing of this to us."

I didn't like his tone and was afraid that my plan was about to fail before it had begun. "I'd call him but he's on the road. Do you really want me to leave and tell him that you wouldn't let me do my job? I'm not just some woman. I'm an officer. I am the wife of the Chi of Earth. How dare you tell me where I can and can't go?" The poison with which my words stung the air shocked me. In the constraints of a society that treads women down, I had always managed to get what I wanted. I wasn't prepared to stop now.

He looked at me in shock. "Apologies, Ma'am." He mumbled. "Of course you can go in. We aren't prepared for a visit mind... I am sure you will find things in order nonetheless..."

"Very well, thank you." I said primly. I nodded to him and made my way through the next set of doors.

"Ma'am, wouldn't you care for an escort?" He asked quietly. By this point he was clearly afraid he might say the wrong thing and send me into another outburst.

"I know my way around, thank you," I told him, hoping that I remembered it from my visits before when it was just an empty shell of a building. I walked off with an air of confidence, clasping one of Abram's electronic note-takers.

I walked into what appeared to be a holding area. There were benches at one end and showers at the other. I noticed with curiosity that there were no shower curtains. I assumed they would bring out screens or something when they were in use. The whole area had a clinical feel to it. It was very clean and white and the lighting was bright. It had the smell that all hospitals have, the smell that is left behind when all germs and bacteria are stripped away.

From here I had a choice. To my left there was a door marked staff area. To the front there was a door to the general hospital. I went into the staff area first. I knew that my actions would be closely monitored through the security systems and I needed to keep up appearances. It was important to ensure the guards lost interest in me quickly so that I could investigate more openly.

Through the door was a grand room. There was art that had clearly been flown in from back home; it was a series of scenes from around our planet. There were glorious sunrises out of the wastelands and paintings of the forests and the colourful array of birds. The pictures were so large and covered of almost every wall. It was easy to think that you were back on Holiteria again. I wondered what the men had to complain about when they were coming to work in such a beautiful and relaxing environment. A series of beverages and snacks was set out on a counter to one side. I poured myself a drink using the touch button programmed dispenser and sat down. I could have sat there all day looking at those images. A few men came in and out, but only the highest-ranking officers. They smiled at me and made polite conversation as was to be expected. I decided that I had stayed long enough and that it was better to get out before a mid-morning break or early lunch brought the masses in.

I picked up my handheld and walked back into the holding area. Two armed guards stood the other side of the second door. Each held a laser assault pen. The laser on one of those was so powerful it would cut straight through a person. The beam could sever a limb from ten metres away. They were precise and required a high level of training. I had never seen one in person before. It was intimidating to know that someone held in their hand something that could destroy me so easily but reassuring to know that these men were theoretically on my side. These men were killing machines like their weapons- accurate and deadly.

They stepped aside to allow me access. I smiled cheerily at them and received a sombre nod in return. Once my focus left them I saw an entirely different world lay out ahead of me.

What I first noticed was the way the floors were caked in muddy footprints. There were three little human children down on their knees with a bucket of soapy water cleaning it up but it was a futile task. Men were constantly coming in with muddy boots and everywhere they wiped they had to wipe again moments later. Their faces looked sunken and their spirits broken. This was my first indication that what I had stepped into was not a hospital at all; it was a prison.

I walked towards one of the grubby little children and saw him flinch as he realised I was approaching him. "Child," I said to him as gently as I could, "would you please show me where you keep your buckets and cleaning materials." His face dropped and fear filled his eyes. He cowered back further and I realised boots were approaching us from behind.

"Ma'am, we generally avoid speaking to the humans," he said matter-of-factly.

"Well," I scolded, turning on him sharply, "in my experience, the workers are the ones who know their way best around the storage cupboards. I am here to conduct an inventory and this is the method I have used in other hospitals. Abram knows how I do things and trusts me. I would advise you to do the same!"

He fell away quickly and rejoined the other guard. We really were in a different world and Abram, as Chi, held a lot of power here.

"Come on then, child!" I barked. He hastily got to his feet and scrabbled towards a cupboard. Once I was confident we were out of earshot, I allowed my voice to soften again. He looked thin and ragged, "How often are you fed?" I asked him.

"We have breakfast every morning," he whispered, then lowered his voice even further and added, "if we have worked hard the day before... Ma'am" he said, copying the greeting he had heard the guards use on me, "please could I get back to work... I don't want to fall behind..."

"Of course," I said kindly. "What's your name?"

"Leo."

"Thank you, Leo. I will be sure to let the guards know how helpful you have been."

He scampered away from the storeroom and fell quickly back to his knees to resume his position cleaning the floor. I put my hand to my stomach, where a small child grew.

I stayed in the cupboard and proceeded to write down quantities of various items from within the drawers and on the shelves. I didn't want to alert anyone unnecessarily. I did plan to tell Abram I had been but I didn't want to run the risk of being thrown out before I had a chance to see what was really happening there.

There were a series of doors that led away from this large room that both the humans and us were traipsing mud through. Hordes of humans were marched through in lines, looking ill and drawn. They were all dressed uniformly; a bright blue tabard covered them from their shoulders to their feet and hung off loosely from their bodies. Their feet were bare in spite of the freezing temperatures. Their jaded expressions were that of prisoners. Each line was led through one of the many large white doors that came off this room. I waited until a group had been marched in and watched for the soldiers marching them to leave. When I was sure they were alone in there, I decided to go in myself.

My heart was pounding as I reached the door. I pushed down the shiny silver handle and strode in confidently. The room was filthy. There were soiled mattresses laid side-by-side on the floor and on top of those thin, sullied blankets were folded neatly. There hardly looked to be enough mattresses for people yet it was clear this room was meant for everyone I saw in it.

The troubled faces of a mass of humans stared back at me, vacantly. It took them a moment to register that I wasn't one of them and then the fear crept slowly across their faces. They stood. Some were so shaky on their legs they were being aided by others who were slightly less shaky. There was a sense of camaraderie in their togetherness.

"As you were..." I told them. They looked at me blankly. "Sit!" I ordered. They responded to the order. It was as if that was what they expected of our kind. They sat down slowly, still unsure of my presence amongst them.

The walls were a greyish white but I supposed they had been bright white initially. There were no pictures or images; just a window caked in mud that let in a little natural light. An austere white light hung from the middle of the room.

I couldn't see any space in which these humans would have kept their own belongings. There was just one chest of drawers by the door. It didn't seem like a medical cabinet, and there were no charts or notes for any of the individuals in the room. It wasn't clear what sort of help, if any, these humans were being given here.

I heard footsteps moving towards the door so I began to rifle through the drawers; they turned out to be full of dirty looking bed linen, so I began counting and adding to my list.

"They did an inspection this morning. There's nothing left to find," one little girl said bravely. Her mother snatched her arm and pulled her back, putting a pale, grimy hand over her mouth.

"She didn't mean to speak... sorry," she mumbled. Her eyes were cast to the ground the whole time. It was so cold in there that I could see the breath leaving their mouths as they spoke.

"Who did the inspection?" I asked the little girl directly.

The woman who had grabbed her, I assumed to be her mother, moved her hand away from the child's mouth and beckoned her to speak. "The guards, Miss. I'm sorry- I don't know which one's which..." The young girl replied, as politely as she knew how to be.

"And what do the guards take?" I asked, inquisitively.

"Our things. Things we managed to bring here with us. But there really is nothing left anymore." she said with an earnest passion.

The footsteps had stopped outside the door and I heard muffled voices. As the door opened one of our soldiers stood there looking in. "Ma'am?" he asked.

"Counting linen," I lied. "Each room the same?"

"Yes, Ma'am. Wouldn't go touching them without gloves though if I were you."

"Duly noted. Thank you." I smiled at him gracefully and left the room.

I felt queasy. The stench of grime and bodies clung to me, yet what truly made me nauseated were the conditions these people were living in. This had happened right under my nose and I hadn't seen it. It was hardly any wonder that the men had drawn within themselves and were unable to talk about their work at home. They must have felt ashamed.

Abram had forced them to do this. He was a persuasive man and charismatic too. He had a way of making everything he suggested seem like the only thing worthy of suggestion. Of course, if Javari was to be believed, and I was inclined to say he was, men who didn't follow orders were executed. 'Accidents' happened to them. That was motivation enough for the soldiers to follow his rules if nothing else was.

"I have finished in here anyway." I turned and walked out of the room.

I decided to step outside into the courtyard to get myself some air.

Chapter Twelve – An Informant

I began to see that Abram had no interest in what had happened to this planet in its past. It dawned on me that his motives were parasitical; he had spotted a chink in the Earth's armour and he was being opportunistic.

What I couldn't work out was why he was bothering to even keep these humans alive. It crossed my mind that maybe he felt there might be something to learn from them, or perhaps he just wanted to break their spirits so that he could rule them too. Either way, it was clear that this hospital was not for healing.

The open courtyard that I was standing in was a ring of mud. The winds were bitterly cold as they swept through but I needed a minute away from what I had seen inside. I stood alone.

"Excuse me, Ma'am" a small voice echoed behind me, "I have been sent to ask you if you would like a drink?"

I turned around to see a young, human woman stood before me. She was slight in frame and her bones jutted out as if it had been a long time since she had eaten a proper meal. Her tabard drowned her petite body. I noticed her eye bore a mark that was almost the same colour as her outfit. It was almost black in the centre and changed to a bluish hue around the edge before phasing into a deep red and fading down to the usual pallor of her skin, which was akin to the shade of milky coffee.

"What happened to your eye?" I asked her.

She shuffled on her feet and looked embarrassed. "I was insolent." She eventually answered.

"I will have a drink, please. Just water."

"Very well, Ma'am." She left. I awaited her return contemplating what insolence she could have exhibited to warrant such a brutal response. I assumed she wasn't dangerous or she wouldn't have been sent out to me alone.

The air seemed to be growing colder by the minute. A hostile wind whipped at my face and I drew my coat tighter around me. I sat down on a thin bench that was sheltered behind a brick built wall and huddled my knees towards my chest.

"Ma'am, is everything ok?" asked the voice I had heard before.

"Yes, quite. Just not as used to this weather as you all are!" I replied as she handed me my water.

She looked at me and smiled. As soon as the words had left my mouth, I realised the lines around her lips were an icy blue and the hairs on her arms stood up. I had read about that as a reaction to the cold that human bodies had developed. It was a technique to capture air particles and hold them next to the skin to help maintain the body's warmth. Her teeth chattered in her head. Regardless of all these physical signs of coldness that I had first missed because of my own internal focus, she stood there as a picture of defiance and told me, "Yes, we are much more accustomed to it."

I was mesmerised by her. She had strength and was brave. I needed to know how her experience here had led her to the bruise tainting her pretty eye. "So what happened to your face?"

"It was as I said, Ma'am. Insolence."

"You don't much strike me as the as the insolent type."

She looked uncomfortable. "I'm not looking to report you. I just want to know what happened." The look on her face made it evident that she didn't trust me. She had no reason to either so I didn't blame her. "I'm the insolent one. My husband doesn't know

I'm here. If the soldiers knew I had lied to them, I'm not sure what would happen."

I don't know what made me tell her this. I wasn't lying. If she had gone and told anyone what I said, I would have been in trouble. There was something about her courageousness in the face of her adversity that made me want to talk to her.

"I really should get back to work." She said. She looked awkward.

I stood up, reached out and gently ran my hand over the contour of her eye. Her initial reaction was to flinch away but as she realised I intended her no further harm, her body relaxed. I took her hand and sat her down next to me. "It isn't right." I told her.

She told me her story.

On arrival, like all humans there, she had been given an injection to treat the damage to her immune system caused by the radioactive isotopes of iodine released by the nuclear explosions. She had been told that the site of the hospital was an area that had been cleared of radiation by the guards and that she would be safe there until more land had been cleared. She was then stripped and showered in the holding hall I had seen upon my arrival here.

She talked of the sense of humiliation of being made to shower in front of all the guards and men and women from her own planet. I could see no reason for inflicting this shame upon the humans. Our culture is liberal. We are much more open to the pleasures of the flesh than we know this planet to be. Even then, being forced into nakedness in the presence of strangers would be a debasing experience. I could only imagine, with my knowledge of the role of sex in relationships and tradition for the majority of cultures on this planet, how demeaning this experience was for the young lady before me.

She had then been put into a blue tabard and thrown into a room that was already filled with several others. She had arrived with her mother but they had been split up during transportation and she wasn't even sure if she was here. They had been briefly reunited again the following morning when they had been rounded up and ushered to a large dining hall by men with sticks.

As she had been prodded into the hall with a group of women, being treated as if they were cattle on a farm, she had glimpsed her mother across the other side of the room. She had run to her and grasped on to her for dear life as any daughter would in such a frightening situation.

The reunion had been short lived; one of the guards had beat her across the back of her legs and laughed as she had crumpled down onto the floor. Her mother had tried to help her up only to receive a sharp blow herself. As she sat there on the floor in a state of disbelief, the guard had ordered her to get herself up quickly and get in line for breakfast. She watched her mother weep as she walked away into the line.

Having caused a commotion by running to hug her mother and then sitting there without eating her food, she drew attention to herself. One of the guards pulled her up roughly and growled at her to explain why she seemed to think herself above the food that was served to her. She didn't know what to say and was frightened so he had shouted to everyone to take note about what happens when you don't do as you are asked and then he dragged her from the room. An example was to be made to everyone that day and it was happening entirely at her expense.

She stood outside an office for what felt like an eternity. Her legs shook uncontrollably. Tears of fear fell silently down her face. Her nose dripped. She began to feel dizzy as the pace of her breathing picked up. She began to think she was going to have a panic attack and tried desperately to catch her breath and slow herself down. Then she was called into the office.

A tall guard stood there. She didn't know who he was but she could tell he was important. He had called her in and stared at her for a long time. She had felt herself shift uncomfortably under his gaze. When he felt satisfied, he had come up to her and moved in closely towards her neck. She remembered feeling his hot, moist breath on her skin and how it had sent a nervous shiver down her spine. Then he grabbed her chin, pulled it upwards and kissed her lips. In a blind panic she had bitten him and he had struck her.

Her lifeless body had been thrown against the door with a tremendous thud. When she woke up she was no longer in his office but in a small, dark cell. She described the water dripping down the back wall and the slimy moss that was growing under it. There was no light and she had had no concept of how long she had been in there.

She urinated, defecated and at times vomited in that room and was left there to lie in it. The pangs of hunger made her stomach roar and her head pounded from the effects of dehydration. Occasionally she heard voices pass by outside but the effects of her exhaustion and hunger made them echo wildly so that she could never focus on the original sound. The harder she tried to listen, the further away the voices seemed to bounce. What felt like a hundred years passed by.

It is amazing where the mind can take you in a situation like that. At times she felt she was going crazy; voices and images danced around her in the darkness. She dreamed and prayed and hoped. Eventually she began to think there was nothing left to hope for. Just when she had given up entirely and resigned herself to dying there, the door opened.

She felt a thud hit her with force straight in her eye and fell to the floor. Something was thrown in next to her and a voice snarled, "Clean up in there."

With the new light streaming through the door, it took her a long time for her eyes to adjust from the darkness. The pain was excruciating and her tears were streaming. She worked hard to force her eyes open and eventually realised it was a bucket and sponge that had been thrown into her room.

She set to work cleaning out the cell. Although she was weak from her maltreatment, she cleaned that cell with a sense of obsession. She had come out alive and she was determined to be resilient and strong. She wanted to be as courageous as she could muster strength for. Eventually, someone returned to collect her.

She was returned to the room she had begun in and started talking to the people she shared it with to determine where they were and what this place was.

She went on to tell me horror stories. People who did not respond to the vaccine given on arrival were simply taken out and killed. A pile of bodies grew just outside the walls of the courtyard. I couldn't see them but it explained a lot about the putrid smell of decay that swamped the air.

She explained how a group of men she had spoken with had been tasked with taking the bodies out and piling them into a hole round the back. They talked of mutilations to the bodies – how they looked as if they had been diced up and put back together again before they were disposed of. If I had hazarded a guess, I would have said that the scientists must have been using the bodies and doing post-mortem investigations on them. Whilst this was tragic, I could see the sense in it. The next story was different; I could see no reasonable explanation for it.

One woman arrived back later than the others one night with horrific cuts across her torso that had been sloppily stitched back together. She had sat shaking in the corner unable to speak. Gradually her shivering subsided and her silence became pained screams. Everyone tried to comfort her but nothing would. One woman sat stroking her hair and singing her lullabies. Another just held her hand. They were simple gestures of kindness but none of them managed to break through to her.

Finally, her wounds became red and angry and the woman's temperature began to soar. They banged on the door and called for a doctor and for help. For a long time, it seemed like they were destined to be ignored. The woman rolled from side to side, clutching herself. She muttered and mumbled, speaking in tongues. When a guard did eventually come, he seemed to be annoyed at the inconvenience and dragged the poor woman out by her hair. She never returned.

She explained how she had heard rumours of something the guards referred to as an 'insemination suite' and of plans to repopulate the human people. It was apparent that there were many unanswered questions here and a lot of half finished stories. It added to the terror these poor humans already found themselves in.

I couldn't listen any more and I desperately wished to make her stop telling me. It was then it dawned on me, though I could ask her to stop talking if I desired, she would have to continue to endure it because this was her life now. I couldn't be so selfish as to stop her when talking to me seemed to offer her some sense of catharsis. So I tried another tack.

"Have you seen your mother since?" I asked her, hoping I might redirect her from the stories whilst still appearing interested.

"No," she replied sadly, "but there is a communication network we have here and I know she is well for now-" She cut off suddenly. "I really should go... I have already said too much."

She got up and left and I made no attempt to stop her.

I was in a daze as I got up to leave the hospital. I walked back into the courtyard and towards the door I had come in through.

Suddenly, frenzied screaming filled the air. It sounded like a wild animal in a trap. Just as suddenly as it started it stopped. Every soldier and inmate in the whole building froze and took note of the chilling silence that followed. The Holiterian soldiers began to move first, carrying on as if nothing had happened, yet looking just a little more dead inside. They began to poke humans, ordering them to get back on with their tasks, and soon the bustle and movement returned and the volume increased again.

I signed out without a word and rushed away from the building and back home. Half of me wanted to turn to Javari's arms and half of me wanted to never see or speak to any man ever again. The man who had tried to kiss the girl, the girl whose name I had never even asked for, could have been any single one of the men I knew. It could have been Abram himself. Or Javari.

The only thing I could do was head home. I needed to be alone and contemplate how I was going to bring this up with Abram. I didn't even know how to begin a conversation with him about what I had done and what I had seen. In my heart I knew I wanted to find a way to end the suffering that was taking place at the hospitals. Unfortunately, in my head I knew I had very little power to do anything.

Chapter Thirteen – Confrontation

It was almost a week before Abram returned.

I spent most of that time in my bed. I felt my health ailing and Javari insisted on sending for a doctor. I insisted against it because I knew they would never find anything; my illness wasn't of a physical nature. I was sick because of what I had seen but I couldn't tell anyone this, as that was a conversation I needed to have with Abram alone. I couldn't have told Javari, no matter how much I would have liked to share what I had done, because he would never have forgiven himself for giving me the information that led to my path of horrific discovery.

Every time I closed my eyes I saw closed doors and heard deathly screaming. Dead humans danced on the back of my eyelids. I think the immense similarities between them and us made it all the more gruesome. Sometimes I saw them as us. I saw every horrific image I had seen since arriving here and so I stopped closing my eyes. I didn't sleep and I barely ate. I tossed and turned in my extravagantly comfortable bed whilst the humans slept on filthy mattresses. Doctors fussed about me trying to make me more comfortable while the sick and the dying were murdered.

Eventually Abram returned. He came bustling into my room, doctor by his side, explaining my ailments and tests that had been run. The doctor checked my charts, took my stats and left the room so that I was left alone with Abram.

"Look at you!" He said.

"I'm fine." I told him.

"You're more than fine. Even though you're ill, you look beautiful! Look at how your body's blossomed in the short time I have been gone!" He came over and put his hand on my stomach. "I hope you are looking after our son?"

It was true. I hadn't really noticed quite how much my body had changed already. I had a prominent round mound where my baby grew within me, my breasts were plump and full and my hair was taking on a purple glow associated with the pregnancy hormones.

"Of course, it's just a shame he will be born in to such a questionable existence," I retorted.

I had planned to fly at him with all the fury that was in my heart. I imagined myself yelling at him, screaming and lashing out. It turned out that my years of upbringing as a submissive woman had ingrained something deeply within me, so that all I could muster was mild disdain.

"Excuse me?" Abram responded, confused.

I went on to explain to him what I had done, where I had been and how just the very thought of this happening as a result of our arrival on this planet made me feel shaken to my core.

By the time I had finished talking he looked furious. His eyes had filled with a terrifying rage.

"Who told you about the hospitals?" He demanded.

"It doesn't matter who told me, what matters is what I saw."

"What matters to me is who told you! It is a breach of their non-disclosure contracts and they will be punished!"

"I... I can't tell you."

He slapped me around the face. It stung and I let out a howl. The door began to open as someone rushed in to check I was all right. "Get out!" boomed Abram's voice and the door quickly slammed shut again. He turned back to me, "talk, woman!"

"Ok," I had to think on my feet quickly now because I didn't want to get anyone into trouble, "you need to calm down. I can't tell you because I don't know. I overheard two men talking outside. They didn't know I was there. This may be our home but it is also your office. It wasn't like they were talking in the street; they were talking at their work. They probably didn't realise I was in." I rambled on until he stopped me.

I couldn't believe that he wasn't offering me any justification or showing any signs of shame after I had told him what I had seen. All he cared about was punishing the man who had told me about the hospitals. The conversation was not remotely as I had planned.

"You're right. This is my fault. I shouldn't have left you by yourself. You need someone with you to ensure this doesn't happen again."

"I don't think that will be necessary."

"It will. You will have a full time bodyguard from my staff. I will also get you a maid. Look at you. You are carrying the most precious thing in the world. I should be looking after you; I shouldn't be getting angry and lashing out. I hope you can forgive me. It is just because I love you and I don't want you to see things that will upset you like this has!"

"I don't need a maid. I'm fine. There are plenty of people here looking after me already. And for what it's worth, I am sorry."

All the anger that had shone brightly in his eyes had been replaced with warmth and love again. I knew he would get me a bodyguard and a maid now, and there would be someone by my side constantly. It would make it very difficult to do anything other than Abram's will. A further visit to the hospitals was entirely out of the question.

He leaned forward and kissed me gently on the forehead. He left the room and I was alone for what was possibly the last ever time.

I felt disappointed. I had planned a great confrontation. I had hoped Abram would show remorse; I dreamed I might convince him to improve the conditions in the hospitals. I hadn't achieved anything, but somehow my conversation with Abram had made me feel better. It hadn't come to a satisfactory conclusion but at least he knew that I knew. It meant I would be able to talk to Javari now. Now that I had told him, I could drift off to sleep for the first time since my visit to the hospital.

Although my sleep was plagued with images of the things I had seen there and the young girl with the bruised eye haunted every moment, it was the best sleep I could have had and when I awoke it was dark outside. Abram was in bed beside me, his arm wrapped gently around me.

I think the baby appreciated the rest too because for the first time, I felt it move. It was a bizarre feeling. My body was being pushed from the inside. I shook Abram awake and silently pushed his hand against my bulging stomach. The biggest smile spread across his face and a huge pang of remorse shot through me, as I remembered how this baby wasn't his.

We both fell back to sleep.

In the morning when I woke up, Abram had already left. I rolled over and was startled to find a man sat in a chair, watching me sleep. I screamed.

"Calm down, Ma'am, please. I'm only your body guard."

It had been decided that four of the best men from the security department would take it in turns to babysit me: Clai, Klijia, Solomai and Javari.

It was ridiculous. I wasn't going to sit there whilst a strange man watched me sleep. It was time I got up anyway, so I went and washed myself, got dressed and went downstairs for breakfast. Clai followed closely behind.

Everyone seemed pleased that I was back up on my feet again and rushed around fussing after me. And then I saw Javari. His face was like thunder. He stared at me. I sat down at the dining table and he got up and walked straight out the room. He obviously knew where I had been.

This icy silence between us went on for three days. He avoided me while Clai was acting as bodyguard. The second day with Klijia was spent in the village, catching up with the women and having clothes fitted to accommodate my rapidly expanding body. The third day was with Solomai. That meant that the next day was Javari's watch. It couldn't come soon enough. I knew he wouldn't be able to ignore me if he had to spend the whole day with me.

Initially he put in a sterling effort to avoid interaction with me. He sat stonily through breakfast, stood to attention outside the door whilst I showered and trooped five paces behind me when I said I wanted to walk and set off in the direction of the forest.

We walked for ages and then I couldn't take it any longer.

I stopped and turned on him.

"Are you going to ignore me forever?" I wailed, getting more and more irate, "talk to me!" I pleaded and pushed him. "Talk to me!" I started throwing my arms around, flailing and floundering like a fish out of water. He grabbed my hands and stilled me before pulling me closely towards him and holding me tightly. "I can't bear to have you angry at me," I sobbed.

"I'm not angry. I was just worried. What you did was dangerous. Imagine if you had been hurt. I would never have forgiven myself!"

"I'm sorry, I had to. I needed to."

"I know, sweetie, I know. But it was such a risky thing to do. You should have told me."

"And you would have stopped me."

"Yes," he agreed, "I probably would."

He continued to hold me like he was never going to let me go. Everything that stood between us melted away until just our love remained. I knew we were going to be alright.

Chapter Fourteen – The Help Arrives

It must have been two days later, because I was sitting with Klijia in the garden admiring the plants, when my maid arrived. I had expected her to be one of the Holiterian women from the village so I was immensely surprised when Abram walked down the driveway with a human walking shortly behind him.

She was an older woman, but not so old as to have lost her looks. Even though she looked as downtrodden as the rest of them, there was something quite beautiful about her. I couldn't quite work out why, but there was something strikingly familiar about her too. Her big, brown eyes and long eyelashes that framed them were reminiscent of something I had seen before. Perhaps a picture? And her skin was a gentle creamy shade of brown that looked fragile and delicate.

Sadness filled her eyes yet she held herself with exquisite dignity and poise and curtseyed demurely when she reached me.

"This is for you," Abram told me proudly. I wasn't sure if he was genuinely pleased with himself for finding her or if he was trying to torment or punish me for going to the hospital by offering me help that would be a constant reminder of what I knew was happening. She was being led by a rope tied to chains around her hands and he passed the rope over to me.

"Thank you." I said tenderly taking her reins. I smiled at her and she dipped her head to look at the floor.

"I thought you would be pleased to know that you could save one," he said with a wicked grin. I still couldn't be sure as to his motives but this wasn't my choice either way. I had a maid and I would be expected to make use of her. If I didn't, she ran the risk of being returned to that awful place anyway.

I led her back into the house and to the kitchen. Here, I untied her. After telling her to acquaint herself with the kitchen, I watched her with fascination as she began to open drawers and cupboards. She looked baffled by the technology we had in the kitchen. She picked up a small metal box with a blue digital screen on the front and turned it upside down. Beans from the lolica plant fell everywhere and she rushed to pick them back up again; her face darkened to a bright shade of red.

"It's a Lolica Grinder," I told her. "Beans go in, powder comes out." She didn't seem any less mystified so I continued, "to mix with water. We drink it." She nodded politely.

Once she had rummaged around under my careful gaze, I suggested she started by making Abram, Klijia and I some lunch. A lot of the foods we had were from back home and obviously not what she was used to cooking with. Some of our foods were native to this planet but I had no idea whether they were things she would have considered food or things humans would have eaten.

"Today, I will have someone come and show you the things we have. Perhaps if you write a list I could send someone to collect some things you would feel happier working with. I would love to try some of your food." I told her kindly.

Still she didn't speak.

"And you can make yourself something to eat too?" I suggested, trying to settle her.

Still nothing.

"Perhaps you don't speak English? Abram told me you did? Do you?"

"Yes, Ma'am" She answered. She spoke begrudgingly.

I had initially thought her silence was shyness but it began to feel like it was defiance. I could never have called her rude because she answered all my direct questions and was putting on a show of manners. She was infuriating though.

"Then you have understood what I have asked of you? And you will make lunch when I find someone to come in and help you? And you will make yourself something?"

"Yes, Ma'am."

"Good, because you look like you need some food!" I said smiling.

"Ma'am, I hope I don't speak out of turn but please don't feel the need to feign kindness with me." She said.

I slapped her.

It wasn't an action I was proud of and I certainly couldn't blame her for resenting having to be here to serve me when our people had been so awful to hers. It had been an instinctive reaction because I wasn't feigning kindness. I was genuinely concerned about the welfare of those humans I had met at the hospital. I was so furious because I had no power and I knew that wasn't her fault. I turned and left the kitchen. Klijia followed me dutifully.

I saw Clai outside and sent him in.

I was about to head back out into the garden when I realised that though there were few things I could do, there was one; I could avoid leaving this woman in a situation with the men who had been ordered to be so vile towards her. I took a deep breath and returned to the kitchen.

For weeks I felt the resentment in every kind word she said to me. I tried and tried to make amends, in all the subtle means I had at my disposal – knowing that I had a bodyguard watching my every move and no doubt reporting back to Abram limited me greatly. Nothing seemed to work. I was beginning to give up any hope of forgiveness and, if I am honest, was becoming increasingly callous and uncaring in my dealings with her because I had gone out of my way to treat her as best I could and offer her a peaceful, better life.

I found it increasingly easy to treat her like she was nothing more than a slave.

Then, a few months after she came into my home, I walked into her room to summon her to help me dress and found her, sobbing silently into her pillow. It was only then that it dawned on me that this woman didn't have a better life; she had lost the life she knew and probably a hundred friends and family that went with it. All I had offered her was a better condition of living than the appalling life that my people had offered her. It wasn't me she hated. It was all of us. And who could blame her?

"You must hate us," I said.

"Yes," she replied candidly.

It was the first honest conversation we had had since her arrival here. Although our words were hostile, there was nothing antagonistic about our tone. We were two women stating facts.

I wanted to tell her that I understood; I wanted to make her see that I wasn't responsible and that I deplored what was happening. I felt like I was beginning to understand this woman. Trying to tell her I could empathise with her suffering would probably only anger her. I left her room and got myself dressed.

Getting dressed was no easy feat with my expanding midriff. Bending down was getting increasingly difficult and I had just reached down to put on my shoe when I felt a sharp twinge shoot through me. I shouted out for Clai, who had been loitering outside my door while I changed. He came rushing in to find me clutching my stomach.

"Are you...?" He asked.

"I think so." I told him. "Is Abram here?"

"No. I'll send for him. I'll get someone else to come here- I think the boss is outside. I er... I think this is outside of my jurisdiction."

He hurried out of the room and a minute later Javari, as the head of security, rushed in. He looked panic-stricken. I was so glad it was him that Clai thought to bring.

"It's alright." I reassured him.

"Are you sure this is happening now?"

"Of course I'm sure! Javari, I'm about to have this baby!"

At that moment, the maid ran in followed closely by Doctor Siriah. I was informed that, although they had spoken to Abram, he wouldn't make it back in time but would be here as soon as he could. Siriah was one of the finest doctors Holiteria had to offer so I knew I was in good hands. And Javari was there.

Birth is a relatively quick affair for us, especially compared to humans. It was excruciating though! In all honesty, I can't recall any specific details about the event. It is amazing how quickly traumatic memories can be blocked in an instant as you hold your tiny baby in your arms. But I know Javari was there, holding my hand while I heard myself yelling at him. I also learnt the name of the maid: Amelia.

Amelia put all of our differences aside the moment my labour began. She was the calming influence in the room that offered me the encouragement and support that made me sure I could do it; even at the moments when I begged for it to stop, she motivated me and made me feel strong enough to do anything.

This women, whom I had slapped and mistreated, who knew that my people were torturing hers, looked me deep in the eyes and connected with me on a primal level: woman to woman. She put my gorgeous little girl into my arms for the first time.

I would love to have said this was the start of a friendship between us but it wasn't.

The next week was a blur of nappies, feeding and a constant state of worry. I worried if she was breathing, if her temperature was right, if she was breathing in Earth germs for which her immune system was not prepared. I insisted the doctors visit her twice a day to reassure me.

In my dreams I would be bathing her and her tiny face would slip under the water. I would wake up in a sweaty state of panic as I imagined scrabbling around desperately trying to get her up again. I had endless moments of anxiety about my skills as a parent. I wanted to do my absolute best to give this child everything she deserved and more importantly, in the interim, I just wanted to be able to keep her alive.

I also felt strangely sad that my purple hue was fading and my hair was returning to its pre-pregnancy silver. It was weird not feeling little feet and hands moving around inside me.

Abram was equally besotted with her. It was Javari, at this special time, for whom I felt for the most; he was not family and with Abram constantly by my side, my maid and the doctor were the only staff permitted to see me.

She had the most perfect rosebud lips. Her eyes were big and dark and looking at them made my heart melt. She could have been lifted straight from a picture book. She was the most perfect little dolly. We called her Esmella. It is the name of a delicate flower with a strong but elegant aroma, found hidden deep in the forests of Holiteria.

I felt more tired than I ever thought possible. It was incredible to look after this astounding little gift that I had been entrusted with but it was a full time job with no rest at night. Amelia did her job and her help was invaluable and Abram assisted at times too. I was Esmella's mother though and a lot of the time, it was only me who was able to comfort her.

This whole change in the dynamic between Amelia and I did give me the confidence, at a quiet moment away from everyone, whilst she was getting me dressed, to ask her a question that had played on my mind for a long time.

"Do you have a daughter?" I asked.

"Yes. Well- had."

She turned and walked away and I didn't push it any further.

Amelia was the one to make the next move. I was sat feeding Esmella and she crept in and sat down beside me.

"She was called Claudia," she began. It took me a while to realise she was talking about her daughter. "She was taken to that prison with me. She's dead now."

I sat, quietly, and let her talk. She talked about how they had been brought there together but separated in transportation. Then her story began to sound strangely familiar. Her daughter had seen her in the dining room and run up to hug her. The guards had hit her and they had been dragged apart. She had seen her daughter be taken away by the guards. She had heard through the underground communications that her daughter had been locked up in a solitary cell.

I wondered whether to tell her that I had met Claudia. I wasn't sure if it would ease her pain or increase it to know that I had seen her, spoken to her but clearly failed to save her. I decided it was best to keep that information to myself for now.

It did occur to me that this was quite a coincidence. Of all the women in that building, I spoke to the daughter and then her mother was sent to my home. A fear crept into my mind that perhaps Abram had seen me talk to Claudia on the surveillance tapes and my mission had played a part in leading to this poor young woman's fate. Had Abram put Amelia here in my home in the hope I would discover the link?

I put the thought quickly to the back of my mind and hoped I never found out the answer.

Amelia knew no details of Claudia's death. Officially it had been classed as an accident but the rumours suggested her death was the direct result of a scientific investigation carried out at the hospital. She stopped talking and I sat there dumbfounded. This woman had truly lost everything.

"Do you know what happened to her?" she asked and her words stung me.

"No." I said, shaking my head, "I'm so sorry for everything you have lost."

We both looked at Esmella. I felt a pang of pain at the thought of losing her. My eyes pricked with tears and I choked down a lump in my throat. This was just a drop of the anguish Amelia must have felt. Amelia looked at her because she knew that now I was a mother I might have some understanding of her feelings.

"Are they doing experiments? Is it possible they could have killed her?"

I didn't have the heart to tell her that I was sure it was true but I equally couldn't bring myself to lie to her. "I don't know much. I am practically under house arrest here, as you know, and Abram doesn't tell me anything."

"Thank you." She said and left me there, holding Esmella close to my chest.

Chapter Fifteen – From Bad to Worse

I was so pleased when Abram went back to work and my bodyguards resumed their duties. I knew that it meant Javari and I would soon have some time together again.

When that day came, he was as happy as I was; I placed Esmella in his arms and watched him with joy as he played with her little fingers and toes and she cooed at him. His manner with her was so natural and seeing them together looked perfect.

Sitting together on the end of my bed, Esmella in his arms and my arms around him, we became the image of the flawless family. I longed for a time when we could be this way properly and not just have to act. We were comfortable together and that was something I could never say about life with Abram.

Esmella began to wriggle so we decided to stretch our legs around the house.

I was debating whether or not it would be appropriate to ask him about Amelia's daughter. I wanted to get answers for myself as much as for Amelia. I was just plucking up the courage to raise the subject when he stopped, looked deep into my eyes and told me he needed to talk to me about something.

Being secluded at home, I had missed a lot of the gossip in the village. He explained to me that the men were back to drinking and even the women were beginning to get wind of what was happening in the hospitals.

Abram, as always, put a spin on things. He began to talk about how dangerous humans could be and used evidence from their historical archives to support his viewpoint. He told them of his visions for the future; he was pulling back from Holiteria so that he could put all of his focus into Earth. He informed everyone that the Government of the People had requested his guidance because he was doing such a wonderful job here. It became clear to me that they were entirely in his pocket and he pulled the strings both here and Holiteria.

I ascertained from his schedules and conversations with Javari that 'pulling back' meant weekly communication meetings with the Government of the People in which he told them how to run their planet and took no advice or guidance from them. He ruled both planets but I am sure it isn't possible to run two worlds, one from afar. He was spread too thinly.

Worryingly, he also decided it was time to shut down the Venus Station. Workers there were to choose between moving to a permanent residence here on Earth or to return to Holiteria. It seemed he was confident in his abilities here and this was no longer a mission of discovery but an official take-over.

Javari and I agreed it was foolish to shut Venus Station down, when it was so perfectly placed for data analysis and to warn us of trouble here on Earth. I suppose that was part of the problem; they could detect trouble on Earth and it was becoming increasingly clear that Abram was responsible for much of it himself. By shutting down the Venus Station, he was protecting himself from Holiterians.

I worried about my parents back home and only rarely got to speak to them. The connection was never totally secure and neither of us ever felt like we could talk freely. I missed them so much but it was clear they had no desire to move here.

The people here seemed pleased that there were such good relations between the Holiterians on Earth and those back on Holiteria. They began to feel like we were two separate people cut from the same cloth and in close allegiance with one another. They liked how Abram spoke of our new arrangement. He had bought their quiet for a while.

What was concerning Javari though was what was going on behind closed doors. Things were getting worse at the hospital. I hardly believed that was possible after what I had seen but I sat and listened.

It is funny the details you remember when someone delivers you bad news. I can remember the room I had that conversation in better than any other room in that whole house. It was a study. A mahogany desk sat facing the door with an impressive bookshelf behind it. On the right hand side, the shelves were filled with an impressive array of literature from this planet. The books were all in hard copy with impressive, leather covers and archaic gold-leafed edges. On the left hand side were 'books' from back home. I have mentioned before that we had a significant edge over the humans on technological advancement. Our stories and information sources were all in the form of digital media. The reader needed simply to put on the blacked out glasses and allow the information to be directly sent into your conscious mind.

I thought it was hilarious the first time Amelia heard about the way we gained our knowledge. She thought it would be possible to brainwash a person with them; she imagined downloading a book into someone's unconscious mind and making them believe it was real. I suppose it just went to show how primitive their understanding of the brain was.

The bookshelf, books and desk were all things that had not originally been on the farm when we had arrived. These were things Abram had brought in from various locations. The curtains, a chintzy, green printed pattern, framed the windows. These had been here before. A set of big, comfy armchairs in a floral pattern, which clashed dreadfully with the curtains, had also been resident there long before we arrived. It was on those chairs that we were sitting to talk.

Javari sat in one chair whilst I sat in the other, nursing Esmella. He had a grave look on his face.

There had been a punishment system set up within the confines of each hospital. Humans that did not obey orders were being taken to the medical rooms. They did not return. Abram had decreed it was essential to understand as much about the human body as possible in order for us to be able to use them as needed and ideally maintain them at our mercy.

He had access to all of the medical research done on Earth already, though he objected to their methods of data collection and the tools used. He had specialist equipment teleported in from Holiteria, so everything the staff there had available to them was top quality.

Then he began to talk of vivisection. The room began to swim around me. I couldn't focus on his words. I felt numb. An image of Claudia came into my mind and I couldn't shake it. Amelia's words filled my ears and I thought they would burst. My memory filled with the noise of that horrifying screaming that I had heard on my visit to the hospital. That could have been what I had heard.

Javari was still talking. I was picking out snippets. Each hospital was allowed to pick out a quota of ten "criminals" to use. They had been strapped to benches in the labs and left there until they were needed. Two soldiers had refused Abram's orders, and he had threatened to put them under the knife to make a live comparison of our anatomies.

Men, women and children were all beaten to increase their productivity and ensure they took their places as slaves in the new world.

He had become a monster. I tried to look back to see at what point things had started to unravel to make Abram the tyrant that he had become. The more thought I gave it, the more I realised he had always been that way.

His arrogant confidence, his manipulation of me and my feelings, his secretive take-over during the revolution- these were all my first experiences of him. It seemed stupid to not have noticed it sooner but they do say 'love is blind'. Perhaps I was too focused on my own upward rise to notice.

The very last thing I wanted was my little baby being brought up in a world that would allow this to happen. I hated the idea of her being brought up by a man that was capable of ordering these things, especially when her true father was a good, kind, honest and caring man.

"We have to stop this," I begged Javari.

"I know, sweetie, we do." he confirmed, "But what we need to work out is how."

There was a knock at the door and Amelia entered. That was the last time Javari and I were able to be alone again that day.

That night at around 2am, there was a knock at the front door and a loud, drunk man stood there, shouting to be let in.

"I wanna talk to that bastard!" He kept yelling, "Come on out of there you son of a bitch!"

I looked out the window to where I had a perfect view of the man below. He was one of us; I recognised him as the husband of the lady that had been running English lessons in the New Town Hall building. Down there in the porch, he slurred his words, threw himself around and looked unfit for anything except perhaps throwing up.

Javari and Clai went down to get rid of him and I stayed at the window to watch the show unfold. It seemed like he wasn't prepared to go without a fight. He was hurling himself into them and the wall and his fists thrashed around indiscriminately. Javari and Clai were having a tough time calming him down. They were stood either side of him, rolling his arms forward at the shoulder, but he was still lashing out with his feet.

They weren't able to move him on as quickly as they had hoped and Abram went down to see what was happening.

"What the hell is this?" he bellowed.

"We are done!" slurred the drunk man, "you can't keep making us do this!"

"I suggest you head back home and stop making a scene before you do something you regret." Abram told him.

The man then started to shout. It woke Esmella and her frightened cry resonated through the whole house. This angered Abram no end and so he lifted his hand, made a strange signal and the next thing I knew, the English teacher's husband was dead.

Abram had silently communicated to the two snipers watching from the roof to finish this poor man's rant. Until that day, I hadn't even been aware that a pair of snipers was constantly on watch around the buildings. It seemed we were protected for extreme attack and yet this incredible defence power was used on a man who had intoxicated himself because he was desperate to stop hurting people. Well, Abram had given him his way out. And it made me realise what he could do to us should he wish.

By morning, everyone else knew it too. Abram was feared throughout the land and yet still respected. It baffled me.

I took Esmella for a walk into the village and heard whispers about it.

"Alcohol is evil. There is a reason they ban intoxicating substances back home."

"Abram would be wise to do the same here!"

"He had it coming to him. It's just his wife I feel sorry for."

I wanted to scream at them! I wanted to tell them they had it wrong and that they had been blinded by Abram, as I once was. I wanted to explain to every single one of them exactly what was happening in those hospitals and why their husbands needed to drink. I had to bite my tongue.

I couldn't stand to be there a moment longer.

"The problem," I mused to myself in the mirror later that day, "is that we have all been dictated to for too long. Our minds are rotten and incapable of independent thinking." It was a thought that stayed with me as I fell asleep that night and was still fresh in my mind the next morning.

Chapter Sixteen – The Final Straw

It wasn't long before Javari had found us a way to be together. He had waited until Abram had made arrangements at one of the hospitals and ordered most of the men of the house to accompany him. He argued that, since the untimely death of one of his soldiers on our doorstep, we needed to show a strong, united front. Javari then ordered the men who remained to be posted outside the house to ensure that nobody got anywhere near Esmella and I.

Nobody questioned it. Javari was head of security after all. I think they were grateful to be outside anyway. The sunshine was streaming down, creating the warmest temperatures we had felt since our arrival. There were masses of birds singing in trees and busy little insects flying around and propagating the plants. It was beautiful to see and I almost envied the men outside; when they were not on watch, they were relaxing in luscious, green grass, reading and sharing jokes and stories.

The scene inside the house was much darker. We had closed all the windows and some curtains to ensure that our meeting was secret. Malachi was coming that morning to speak with us. It was just the three of us in the house, except for Amelia who was there to serve us silently as we required.

When Malachi arrived he had aged. His face had grown haggard and deep lines of worry ran through his brow. I embraced him warmly when I saw him and he looked at me kindly but there was a deep sorrow and regret in his eyes. Amelia brought us all a lolica drink and then I dismissed her.

"I'm increasingly concerned by what is happening here. Life at home is not as good as it should be and people are saying Abram is just using the Government of the People as puppets for his own agendas. The things that are taking place here are sickening. We all know Abram has an art for sophistry but the people he preaches to don't seem to see it. He needs to be relieved of his power."

There were no niceties or small talk. He went straight in with what he had to say and what he had to say was shocking but it was not something either Javari or I could take issue with. The only way to stop Abram was to physically put an end to his tyrannical reign here. We spoke euphemistically but there was nothing subtle about our words. It was semantics, but it made us feel better about the task we had to undertake.

We didn't discuss the details initially. We simply discussed the repercussions and what would happen once he was removed. Questions were flying and then Malachi spoke words that would change my path forever:

"As the wife of the Chi, traditionally you would have no power once he was defeated. As the wife of the Chi, who bore his heir, everything is different. Admittedly Esmella is a girl, however, in these changing times, I think we can overlook that. Because she is Abram's daughter, should his death occur accidentally, by our own laws you could take the seat of power in guardianship for Esmella until she comes of age herself." He put an unnatural stress on the word 'accidentally' and it made me feel uneasy.

Javari and I glanced nervously at each other. "Is there something I should know?" Malachi asked suspiciously.

"No," I answered a little too quickly. In the silent moment that passed between us, Javari and I both knew that our secret must go with us if we were to shape this new world in our own, better way.

"Very well then," Malachi went on, "let's formulate a plan."

After a great deal of hushed conversation, of which my input was minimal, we were all in agreement that his death needed to look like an accident.

The main issue we had in each scenario we considered was the snipers who watched him and his home constantly. It meant that his 'accident' had to happen at night, under the cover of darkness, where we wouldn't be seen causing it.

In the end it was decided that we would wait until a night when Javari was on body guard duty. He would wait for Abram and me to go to bed, where I would crush a sedative into the glass of water that he drank every night like clockwork. The tablet wouldn't be so much as to knock him out, but enough to ensure he was malleable and open to persuasion. Malachi was confident that he could get access to the right pill for the job.

Once he had fallen asleep, Javari would go downstairs and join in a game of poker in the drawing room with the other men to ensure that there was no possibility of him being open to accusation.

My job would then be to gently lift him up and guide him towards the staircase where I would push him down. Nobody would suspect a doting wife and so it would be assumed to be an accident.

Malachi, upon hearing the thud, would be first on scene. He would be on hand to twist Abram's neck should the fall have not seen an end to him.

I was concerned as to the logistics of the operation. Abram was significantly larger than me and I worried that if he wasn't willing to get himself up, the plan would fall apart before it began because there was no way I would be able to lift him unaided. Malachi assured me that the tablet he planned to get would make my task easy.

I wanted to know how he could be so confident. I noticed an exchange occur between Javari and Malachi when I asked that question and it made me uneasy. I pushed on.

"How? How can you be so sure?" I repeated.

Malachi looked back at Javari who nodded and waved his hand before him in a gesture that gave Malachi his blessing to continue. As soon as he began to talk, I immediately regretted my curiosity.

Much research had been done on the histories and practises of Earth and its various cultures. It seemed one had sparked a particular interest in Abram. It was one that he had discussed with me in the past on a dark, dreary night as we laid together in bed. It was a work published by Wade Davis on the mythological phenomenon of zombies.

He had learnt about zombies and their connection to voodoo religion. He made himself quite the expert and fascinated me with horror stories of men and women that returned from beyond the grave. I had many a nightmare-plagued sleep thanks to his stories. What he found most interesting though was Davis' information on how zombies could be created. He had read this and many other works.

The last time we spoke of this topic, he explained how a combination of drugs including tetrodotoxin could produce a trance like state that appeared akin to death. Voodoo priestesses would then keep the zombies in this state giving a second drug to their zombie slaves to induce a psychotic state in which they would do whatever was required of them. To stop him going on at me, I had then told him that this was no topic of obsession to share with a woman and that he needed to stop talking about such things.

He had scooped me up in his arms at that and held me like a precious flower. He apologised, kissed me and promised to mention it no more. He had been true to his word.

What I hadn't realised was how his fascination had continued to play on his mind.

Malachi explained that his interest in this had led to some pharmaceutical experimentation on inmates at the hospitals. The ingredients suggested in his reading were not all available to him and he wasn't sure if the writing was factual anyway, as many sources he read had been discredited. He gave his medical team everything he had at his disposal and set them to work creating a medicine that, when introduced to the blood stream, would put prisoners into a deep, deathly sleep.

Once this was succeeded, the second phase was to create the second drug. It had taken the best minds on the planet weeks, but they cracked the code and released a potentially deadly secret.

Abram had begun to choose his slaves. They were all to be men and women of high fertility. Women past child-bearing age were of no use to him and were to be disposed of.

Malachi was as unsure of his motivation as everyone else. Abram kept his secrets close to his chest. What was clear was he was planning on expanding the human population and if the humans weren't prepared to reproduce of their own accord, he was prepared to make them do it by his will.

He had also invested a lot of time on genetic research to ensure that the effects the radiation had on their bodies was suitably reversed by the treatment he had given them. He wanted them breeding healthy offspring, rather than those with radiation related deformities.

The plan was, once everything was set properly in motion, to show a few of the humans his pharmacological slaves, in the hope of scaring them witless so that they would do as he asked willingly. He was very clever at making people succumb to his desires. The threat of becoming his zombie would easily have seen most humans do anything, I was sure. So I knew he needed to be stopped before this plan was thrown into reality.

I couldn't believe the hideous lengths Abram had gone to. His plans were immensely dark. I despised his behaviour and the thought of him coming home to me tonight, taking me into our bed, touching me... it made me feel as if I was drowning; a heavy, dark body of water was crushing down on me and I couldn't breathe.

As much as the idea of murdering him myself appalled me, I wanted to do it immediately to avoid the future he foresaw.

I was reassured that Malachi could supply me with the drugs needed to get the job done. This gave us the first part of our plan.

Killing Abram would put me in power. This we knew. What we didn't yet have in place was a plan for phase two. For this, we need to discuss what it was we wanted from this planet.

For me, it was easy. I wanted a good quality of life for my daughter, one where a woman could grow up strong and independent. I wanted her to enjoy this beautiful planet. I wanted to rule. I wanted all the power that had been taken from me in my life.

Javari wanted life here too. Our planet back home was too difficult for him. It was alive with memories of his first love. He loved me now but he would never forget the tragic loss of his childhood sweetheart who died to save him. Life here was easier for him because he could fill it with his own new memories of love and escape the old, painful ones.

Malachi also wanted his life here on Earth. He was getting older now and wanted a place where he could relax and live out his days. To him Earth seemed like the perfect place to do that.

It was decidedly clear that we all wanted to maintain our life on Earth. This was where our lives were now.

It was decided that our best course of action was to wait. We needed time to think through the second part of our plan and see how everything would fit together. We all went our separate ways that evening and our plan was the only thing to think about.

Chapter Seventeen – A Sudden Death

For your own sake, I hope you have never had to kill someone. It filled my mind every second of the day; I pictured the scene in my mind. Sometimes it ran perfectly and other times it unravelled and fell apart. The thing that drove me during that time was fear.

That night Abram wanted to take me passionately the way he used to. It was rough and intense.

As he ripped my clothes from my body, I thought about how I would have to kill him just a few days later and my mind began to spin. I wasn't sure if I could do it. The water was crushing me again and I couldn't catch a breath. I had to keep up pretences for Abram. He couldn't know I was upset. I wanted to curl up in ball until everything was over but I couldn't because of my integral role in his death.

I shut my eyes and let my thoughts drift me away. Eventually, when everything was over and Abram had drifted to sleep, I curled myself up in his arms. My mind wrestled with itself over this. He repulsed me yet for some reason I was drawn to him. There was no choice but to kill him but I still didn't hate him. I just hated what he was doing.

I fell asleep in his warm, comfortable arms.

I woke up in his cold, stiff arms.

Abram was dead.

Chapter Eighteen – The Hunt Is On

I woke up earlier than usual because Abram's arms were as cold and firm as a stone statue. They were restricting my movements, chilling me to the core and making me uncomfortable.

I didn't wake up quickly. I drowsily pried myself free of his grip and rubbed my eyes. They struggled to open as a bright sunlight shone in through the window. The sky was a brilliant clear blue. As my eyes began to focus I realised that the clouds had quite simply fallen from the sky and had settled around the farmyard. It was a ghostly, misty haze.

I moved and my leg came into contact with Abram's. I felt that icy chill seep into my bones again. I started. I knew that coldness. It was the gentle embrace of death.

Suddenly I was alert. My mind raced. He looked so peaceful and still. I didn't know who had done this. It wasn't our plan. Had someone done it so that I wouldn't have to? Had he died of something natural? I was confused. I didn't know whether to scream or run downstairs. I couldn't remember how a person acted when they discovered the shocking death of a loved one.

It turned out I didn't need to remember. My body instinctively took over for me. I began to whimper and shake. "Help me!" I cried out. I threw myself at his body and shook him. "Wake up!" I yelled, "Please! Wake up!" And when he didn't I put my head on him and cried.

Solomai rushed in. He was my bodyguard that day. He was by far my least favourite of all of them and I hadn't warmed to him in the slightest. He took his work too seriously and never allowed me any freedom. I was glad to have him there beside me though. I knew he would take control and tell me what to do.

The following few minutes seemed to last a lifetime. A steady stream of men arrived in our room. Solomai lifted me gently from Abram and carried me into the dressing room. He then sent Amelia in to dress me. She didn't say a word.

I was half way through putting my clothes on when Esmella filled my mind. I chastised myself for not thinking of her sooner but I was in a state of shock. I rushed out of the room, leaving Amelia standing there dazed and ran to Esmella's nursery. She slept soundly in her Moses basket, oblivious to what was unfolding around her.

I picked her up and pulled her tightly to me. I breathed in her delicate smell.

Amelia followed me in with the rest of my clothes and continued to dress me. She still didn't speak. Once she had completed the task of dressing me, she tenderly wiped away tears from my eyes, straightened me up and said simply, "You're ready now."

She was right. I took Esmella and walked back into the room. By that time Malachi and Javari had both arrived and an emergency meeting had been called. I was advised my attendance would be required. A post-mortem had been ordered. I desperately wanted to speak alone with Javari and Malachi beforehand to find out what happened.

"Malachi, is it possible we could get a moment alone before we meet with everyone? I could use a friend right now." I told him desperately hoping he would understand what I wanted.

"I'm afraid we need him first," replied one of the doctors. "He needs to witness the post-mortem, and we need ascertain the cause of death as quickly as possible. If you don't object, may we move his body?" Then, as an afterthought, he added, "We are very sorry for your loss..."

Everyone moved out as Abram was carried from our room. They were all so focused on their task that nobody seemed to notice that Javari stayed behind with me. I wasted no time because I didn't know how long we would have together.

"Did you do it?" I asked.

"I was going to ask you the same. It wasn't part of our plan."

"Malachi then?"

"It seems unlikely. He was the one who formulated our plan in the first instance. And I guess it wasn't you?"

"No. It was as much as a shock to me as to you," I replied. "Possibly more so, I had to wake up to it!"

I was insulted by his accusation even though I had just done the same to him. I wasn't prepared to jeopardise everything. I began to think that perhaps it was just a natural death. He was a young man but he had a lot of stress in his life. It was not out of the realms of possibility that he had just passed away in his sleep.

We sat there in silence for a long time.

Solomai's presence pulled us from it as he came to confirm that the post-mortem had been concluded. I was shocked. We must have been sitting there for a long time! I realised that at some point during our exchange I had passed Esmella to her father and she slept soundly in his arms. It passed my mind that Solomai might find this scene he had walked into bizarre.

"...and?" I asked.

"It isn't good news I am afraid. Murder. He was drugged. I am sorry." He said he was sorry yet he looked at me suspiciously. I thought that I might have imagined it. I really didn't think he looked very sorry at all.

"Malachi has ordered that the meeting commence now. He said I was to request your presence, Ma'am."

I felt uneasy about way Solomai had addressed me. I knew I hadn't any hand in Abram's death but I felt oddly guilty. Was it possible to kill some just by planning to do it? It certainly felt like it was.

I called for Amelia and handed her my sleeping child. I went to attend the meeting. It was my first on this planet and I felt nervous. I used to be a part of these things but since our arrival here, particularly since Abram became Chi, my role was not a profess-ional one and I had forgotten what it was like to be involved. I had the added pressure now of knowing that I might be headed for power myself; I needed to make a good impression and show everyone that I wasn't just some stupid woman. I wanted the men to take me seriously.

The room was quite different to the offices I was used to on Holiteria and Venus. Holiteria was complete with state of the art technology, communication systems, shiny metal furniture and exquisite paintings and decor. It was a grand room. The conference room in the Venus Station was modelled very much on the one at home.

This room was so much more earthly. A long wooden table ran down the centre of the room and chairs covered in red leather lined either side. There was very little technology in there other than the communication links to Venus and Holiteria and a teleportation hub. It seemed less professional and more homely and yet it somehow made me feel less comfortable. Luckily for me, my job was largely led and dictated by Malachi.

Malachi decreed the first order of business to be reassigning leadership. He spoke of a spacecraft floating through space with no captain and its crew all pulling in different directions. The craft ended up plunging into a black hole. His analogy was to reassure the men that we were in a delicate time, when we needed to have one leader to whom we could all look to for guidance. They nodded enthusiastically. The problem was I knew that the leader was me and I felt ill-equipped to captain a space craft, never mind be appointed Chi to an entire planet.

Surprisingly the men put up very little opposition to my leadership. I thought they would object vehemently to a woman taking power when they had been raised in a culture of patriarchal leadership. I suppose they were just so unhappy with Abram's orders that they were relieved. I suspected they realised that Malachi championed me as the natural, right choice by marriage and as I bore an heir. I think they assumed Malachi would be my puppeteer.

Once it was decided that I was acting Chi, I was asked what the next order of business was to be. I was confused. Part of me wanted to know who had killed Abram but another part of me was afraid of the answer. If I set men into investigating it, then they could find Javari or Malachi guilty and then I might be forced to put a punishment on them. I didn't want that. So the second order of business was having Malachi and Javari work together to find the killer. I hoped that would solve my problem.

After this, I set Clai and Solomai to increase security for Esmella and I. I feared we could be targets if anyone saw that there could be a weakness now Abram was gone. They had the whole security team at their disposal. Extra snipers were to be put around the farm too. I ordered Javari to take night duties. He was to stay each night in my room to ensure that nobody tried to poison me in my sleep. Klijia would take night duty in Esmella's room.

Josiah and Samson were my husband's two most trusted advisors. Whether they loved him or hated him, they knew him better than anyone. I asked them to make arrangements for a traditional funeral. They agreed willingly.

Once I had these things sorted, I looked to Malachi to see if anything else needed sorting. He told me I had covered everything for now and advised another meeting be called later in the day. I agreed and dismissed the men, who seemed relieved to see Malachi advising me. He had no claim to Chi himself but he would clearly have been everyone's first choice, so they were glad to know he would be the trusted voice.

I thanked Malachi and told him I would take some time alone. It was then, when I decided to take some air walking in the garden that I learnt what everyone was saying about me.

Two men, unaware of my presence, were talking candidly to each other in the courtyard.

"You think she did it?"

"If she didn't then Malachi did."

"Thank God! Someone had to do it."

I knew immediately that they were talking about Abram's death. Fear struck my heart as I realised suspicion was on me; then I thought carefully about their words. They weren't angry or upset. They didn't seem to care if Malachi or I had committed murder. They just seemed pleased that Abram's reign of terror was over. It was then I knew, as long as I undid some of the damage Abram had done, I would have these men on my side.

Javari, it turned out, was not as happy as I gauged everyone else to be. As I continued on my walk, he came marching up to me looking like thunder.

"Why did you take me off security?" He demanded.

"I didn't! You are on my night watch duty." I stammered confused.

"Great. I get to be your sex slave by night and by day I am doing detective work to find out who killed your evil husband. I am a security officer!" he was practically yelling at me by now.

"I put you on night duty because I trust you and I love you and I thought you would want to spend time with me!" I yelled back with equal ferocity.

"I do, I do. I'm sorry," he said much more gently this time.

"This is all a lot for me," I told him honestly.

"I know," he said and he held me tightly.

He lifted up my chin and kissed me tenderly. "What I don't understand," he said, "is why you would have me investigate Abram's death? There are men much better for the job."

"Because I genuinely have no idea what happened!" I explained, "and-"

"And you think it might have been me?" He interrupted.

"I suppose it crossed my mind."

He looked annoyed again. It didn't have the same intensity that this conversation started with but he definitely wasn't pleased. "But I told you it wasn't me!" he said. He turned and left me standing there.

Chapter Nineteen – What now?

I loved the idea of being in charge when it was just an idea. When it became reality there were lots of things I hadn't considered. I didn't know where to begin. I was sure there were lots of things to be done and lots of tasks to delegate, but I didn't know what they were.

I couldn't officially become Chi until the Government of the People back at home had agreed and an official ceremony had taken place. This would take a while and during this time, I could not make any public speeches. For all intents and purposes, I was Chi though. I was able to make changes and take power. It was a big responsibility.

Although the Government of the People were to agree my position, it quickly became clear to me how much input Abram had taken in the running of Holiteria. It seemed I now had that to deal with too. All of the official decisions of the planet were run past me first. I wondered how Abram had ever found time for all of this.

Luckily for me I had Malachi firmly on my side. I knew Javari was there too but he was still a little off with me because I questioned him over the death of Abram.

The search for the killer continued and it was making me a nervous wreck. Everyone was a suspect. I spent hours wondering if my daughter and I were targets. Was Abram the only hit on the list or were others to follow a similar fate? I jumped at my own shadow and refused to walk anywhere without Esmella by my side and a team of bodyguards surrounding us. It was a frightening time and I was constantly anxious.

For all the things I didn't know I had to do, there were some tasks that were essential. I had to reshape our plan for Earth. The first thing that needed to happen was the dissolution of the hospitals.

I wasn't stupid. I realised we had treated the humans abysmally and there would be a lot of anger and resentment towards us. Angry people who aren't kept oppressed will organise themselves and fight back. Despite this, I knew I didn't want to return home again. Here I was a powerful woman in charge. At home I would be another faceless widow; good for nothing, ignored by society and without a voice. I couldn't willingly return to that. Not when I could shape a future for Esmella and myself where women can be strong and fiercely independent. Whether to stay or not wasn't even a consideration so I needed to set to work here and make an impact.

It wasn't possible to complete my task overnight. I decided to focus on one hospital at a time. Everyone was briefed. I was to speak to the entire population of inmates and explain what was happening. They would then be moved to a compound of houses, fenced off and closely guarded by our soldiers but with freedom to rebuild their lives and access to proper medical consultation from our excellent teams. They would not be permitted to leave the compounds. This was for our benefit as much as theirs. Radiation levels on much of the planet were still higher than human bodies could handle. They were safe on our cleared compounds; we could keep an eye on them there and ensure we maintained power.

I expected the humans to be relieved but I acknowledged that feelings of animosity might remain. I wanted to show them that I could be trusted and that our people were on their side too. To do this, I needed to be hands on in my approach to fixing things.

The men were all aware of my new position within our hierarchy and they had spoken with their wives too. They were pleased that I was already taking action to disband the hospitals and set up more humane areas for human residence. They hoped this meant their days of torture and abuse could be over. I used the buzz that my reign had created to recruit some women from the village to assist me with the task ahead of me.

I asked Clai to arrange for our safe transportation to the hospital and I went there with fifteen women early the next morning. I briefed them as best I could on the way there but I knew they would be horrified by what they saw.

Before I addressed the entire population of the hospital, we worked room by room taking one person each at a time. We gently wiped away the layers of mud and grime that had built up on their weary, aching bodies. We cleansed their hair and cut matted knots away. We clipped their toenails. We treated them gently and with respect. They said very little to us and they were confused.

It wasn't an easy task. Their bodies were filthy and the smell that hung off them was difficult to displace with just buckets of warm soapy water. We tried hard to mask our disgust at the task we were doing and make the humans feel valued and loved. It was a tall order but our hearts were in a good place and we genuinely believed we were doing something for good.

We had worked our way through the inhabitants of nine of the rooms. We had planned to stop for a lunch break after room ten. I was leading a dejected, broken man to my pan of warm water when a scuffle broke out.

I turned around and saw a human woman tearing savagely at the hair of one of the women accompanying me, Karina. The human's hand were clasped tightly around a clump of hair whilst her other hand scratched slices from her face. The human had a frenzied, mad look in her eyes. She was filled with hate.

"You think you're Mother Bloody Theresa!" she shrieked at the confused lady she was attacking. I rushed forward and tried to prise her away; I grabbed at her arm and her grip released with a handful of shiny, silver hair. Karina let out an immense scream of pain. Everyone else in the room froze in a state of shock.

Three guards rushed over to disable the woman but she had locked herself onto Karina and was refusing to budge.

The other humans in the room saw this unfolding and an expression of hope shone in their eyes. One man stood up and yelled "get her!" with all the venom and hate he could muster. They all began to move forward with wild confidence. They outnumbered us and they knew it. They found courage in their group and it was building with tremendous speed. To begin with they were just encouraging the action. It wouldn't have been long before someone else joined in on the attack and a small riot would begin.

There was nothing else to do: I picked up a heavy, metal pan and brought it down hard on her head. She fell to the floor and Karina collapsed into my arms. The humans stopped dead where they were and began to sink back slowly into the crevices of the room.

"Thank you," Karina sobbed. "Thank you so much!"

I looked down at the lifeless body on the floor at my feet. There was a stream of dark red blood running from her nose. Her eyes rolled back in her head.

"Get her out of here!" Clai ordered.

"Get them all out of here." I demanded as I ushered the women out of the room.

If they hadn't been afraid of us before, they certainly were now. I knew I was offering them a better life and something towards a way out of this hell. I also knew I had inadvertently sent a very clear message- I wasn't to be messed with any more than my late husband had been.

Clai and the other soldiers were furious with the occupants of room ten. I had given no orders but the bloodthirsty nature that Abram had instilled was still within them. Three men were sent in and given ten minutes to exact their revenge before they were pulled out, covered in human blood. This wasn't what I had hoped for today but I think it showed the women that, whilst it isn't right to treat the humans as Abram had, it also wasn't a viable option to set them loose amongst us.

After reassessing the situation, we decided it would be more productive to use the humans we had already cleaned up to clean the remaining ones. I didn't deem it safe enough for us to continue after what had happened and Karina was still in quite a state.

I didn't let this deter me from taking a 'hands-on' attitude though. Whatever we wanted the future to look like on this planet, if I was to keep the humans alive then I would need to have them on my side.

It had crossed my mind on a few separate occasions that we might stand a better chance of making a life here without the natives. There weren't a huge number of them and the ones that remained were weakened anyway. Abram had kept them alive though and clearly appeared to have plans to increase their numbers too, so until I had a clearer understanding as to why that was, I needed to keep my options open. It would be hard to justify a massacre and keep your own team on side too anyway- especially as it would be them who would have to carry out the dirty work.

I decided my new role would involve helping assign individuals to buildings within the new compound. All inmates were instructed to make a list of the names of any kin they had within the hospitals that they would wish to live with once released. These lists were cross-referenced by Amelia and houses were allocated.

The area for the compound was selected from an area already standing, so no building work was required other than the erection of a tall fence dug deep into the ground around the perimeter. We had chosen an area with a lot of multi-storey flats and small houses within a relatively small area of land. It was clearly going to be easier to maintain control and order if the space to control was minimal.

I went and inspected the compound on the day before we were ready to move people in and it was good. It wasn't extravagant or luxurious but every man, woman and child would have a place to live with a roof over their heads. There were some areas where trees still stood and flowers grew. Grass and weeds sprouted up in a large, grassy park area that had been included and some buildings would be left vacant and unassigned to allow humans to set themselves up shops once they began to get organised.

Seven Holitarian men and three Holitarian women had been chosen to form a council for this compound. They were in charge of punishing bad behaviours, assigning empty buildings to people who required them and generally running the village and approving changes. Everyone living there would be accountable to them and they would report to and be accountable to me. I was very pleased with the system.

On the day the people were due to arrive, I positioned myself at the entry gate. Every one of them would collect the key to their house and the map to show them the location from me. Amelia had spent several painstaking hours preparing this for me and she would be there by my side to show that good relations between races were possible.

The day passed relatively smoothly. Several guards were on hand by the entrance with me and several more were stationed at various points inside. They were all heavily armed. We couldn't risk trouble at this stage.

The only issue that arose was right at the beginning when people were so desperate to get into the compound they began to crush each other and push and trample. The guards formed a line in front of them and walked slowly forward to push them back. The people at the back of the crowd continued to push forward and a back and forth, wave like motion ensued.

Malachi instructed Jomia to fire a warning shot into the air. The crowds screamed and surged back again quickly.

"Stop exactly where you are!" I boomed over their stunned, silent heads. "We will do this one at a time in an orderly fashion. Anyone who cannot follow this simple instruction should be warned: Jomia here has been instructed to shoot to kill next."

A quiet murmur rifled through the crowd and Jomia stood strong and fierce.

After that, things ran like clockwork.

Chapter Twenty – Handmaid's Confession

Things had been going well in the new compounds and three of the hospitals were shut down successfully already. I was beginning to relax into my new position and was enjoying life again. I felt confident that I was making a difference, for the better this time. Malachi had also informed me that in the next few weeks, I would be able to have my official ceremony and make a public announcement to the people of both races.

Javari and I had been getting on much better and he seemed to have forgiven me for thinking he might have been involved in Abram's murder. The case had still not been solved but it hadn't really been a priority for anyone. Abram's tyrannical rule had ended and most people were relieved. His murderer could have been any of a great number of people here. In fact, everyone was a suspect for one reason or another.

Javari had maintained night watch duty in my room. It was the one time we could pretend to be a normal couple. Our relationship remained a secret from everyone because it was important nobody suspected I had cheated on Abram. My whole rise to power as Chi depended on my daughter, Esmella, being Abram's natural heir.

We led in bed at night, faces close, discussing the events of the day and gossiping about things that had happened in the village; Mikea's wife had been spotted spending a lot of time with Siriah, one of the medical officers. Mikea had to answer to Siriah because he was his superior so there wouldn't be much he could do about it anyway, if it turned out to be true. I told Javari that I felt sorry for Mikea. He seemed like such a nice young man. It was conversations like these that made us feel normal. We enjoyed those moments together. Quiet moments where Javari could trace his finger gently down my side or where I could rest my head on his bare chest.

It was a lazy Sunday morning when Malachi burst in and interrupted us. Esmella was out with Clai for a walk; he was fast becoming our most trusted security guard and he doted on her. Javari and I had decided we would make the most of finding ourselves alone with no reason to get out of bed so we were not pleased at the interruption. Malachi seemed strangely animated though and he begged us to follow him quickly.

We both threw on some clothes and followed him into Amelia's room.

"She has something to tell you," he explained.

I gave her a quizzical look and she averted her eyes. Guilt was all over her face. I looked at her, there on the floor. Her hands were tied tightly behind her back and her feet were tied at the ankles. She was in a kneeling position and looked like she could have been praying. She probably should have been.

"Go on," Malachi told her.

And she did. She went on to explain that she had been cleaning in Abram's study a few days before he was found dead. She had been intrigued by the handheld that he spent a lot of time dictating notes into. She had noticed how he always stopped dictating and reverted to typing whenever anyone else was around.

It took her a while to work out how to activate it but once she had, his most recent document appeared before her. It was written partly in our own language, which of course she couldn't understand, but there were several parts scribed in English too. Having seen Abram use it many times before, she knew the handheld took its instructions via highly developed voice-activated controls and so she asked it if it would translate the whole document. It took her a few attempts to get the command sequence correct but it didn't take long and she had the whole document in English. What she had read had shocked her.

She was already angry with Abram because it had become very clear that he was the one in charge and that he was responsible for what went on behind the closed doors at the hospital. She had lost her daughter to his experimentation and she couldn't feel anything but hate towards him. Fury ravaged her and every day she became more and more of an empty shell. She hated Abram for all of this.

The contents of the document furthered her revulsion.

The screen before her was documenting the murder of the first survivor found by us, the pregnant woman who had been pulled into my cart, coughing and spluttering on that dark night on our journey here. Abram had ordered her to be killed by Siriah. For all her suffering before we met her and her valiant fight to survive, she met her end at his hands and those of his medical team. They were under strict instructions to learn everything they could from her anatomy and anything that might be useful to aid our survival here.

All of their findings were right there for her to read. She explained it had made her feel physically sick to see this poor woman's murder described in such a cold clinical way. Something interesting had caught her eye though. Siriah had discovered antibodies in the placenta that were being passed on to the baby to ensure its survival here until its own immune system was active. They had stored those antibodies and had successfully used them in a vaccine, and as a treatment, at a later date; the date when Jomia became ill and made a sudden miraculous recovery.

I put my hand onto my arm at the site where I had been vaccinated shortly after Jomia's health had been restored. It was now clear what I had been vaccinated with. There was something upsetting about knowing that a baby had been killed so its life-saving antibodies could be used to save the people who killed it. I had no time to mourn however as Amelia was already moving on with her story.

Not long after that night, Abram had decided that all men would be vaccinated and the entire batch of antibodies was used up. He had planned to impregnate further women, allow them to birth their offspring in hospitals set up by him, and the placenta would be delivered and kept by the medical teams to ensure we had a constant supply of vaccine to ensure our health here on Earth.

Suddenly it was becoming clear to me why Abram wanted to keep them alive. We needed the native resilience to disease that they had built up through thousands of years here. Our immune systems wouldn't cope without their assistance. I thought of the women and children that had been brought here that, as yet, had not been vaccinated and I knew we needed to find a way to rectify this as soon as possible. I didn't want to risk losing my subjects before I had even become their official Chi.

It seemed cold and heartless to be thinking these thoughts in the midst of the horrifying disclosure Amelia was making. My priorities now had to be ensuring the safety of the people in my charge; the men would never forgive me if I let their women die.

Abram had also documented the surprising resilience shown by the human race. It had been hard to break their spirits and, as Karina and I had learnt the hard way, even now some of them still held that spark of fight in them. I thought perhaps the fact that their planet was destroyed and that they had very little to lose made them fearless.

Amelia then went on to explain more. It seemed that Abram had been responsible for setting off the series of nuclear explosions that had ruined earth in the first place. His notes implied he had been planning for it for a long time. He wanted it to look, even to the humans, like it was a disaster caused by the humans themselves. He believed that the survivors would blame politicians. This was a clever plan, as the people in seats of powers would have been in the high profile locations that would be destroyed. Nobody would be able to prove it was not war. It was a flawless plan.

He had then set an explosion on the Isle of Wight, a small island off the south coast of England. There was not a high population there but he wanted it to be used as a base from which we could easily access mainland Britain and spend time to set ourselves up once we arrived on the planet.

This was an insane amount of information to be taking on board. I couldn't decide if I despised Abram or if I was in awe of him. The fact that he was able to construct this plan alone and then manipulate everyone enough to secretly deploy it was impressive. He quite clearly had a dream of starting a better life here, on a planet much larger and more hospitable than our own.

Javari reached out to me and clasped my hand firmly in his. I felt his strength transfer across to me and some of my energy was restored. It was reassuring to have someone to lean on when I was learning such awful things about the man I had shared my life and my bed with.

Amelia confirmed his end goal. He hoped to rule not only Earth but control the Government of the people at home as well. He was power hungry, not just to be a ruler across nations, but across galaxies.

Malachi waved Abram's handheld. "I've read all the information this handmaid has told me and she's correct." He confirmed.

"Amelia," I said, looking down at her carefully, "what did you do with all this information?"

"I saw red. I wanted to launch myself at him, kicking and screaming. I wanted to find a weapon and shoot him down where he stood. I wanted to make him feel pain, to hurt him. But I knew that if I really wanted to stop him, I needed to be patient. So, I waited."

She stopped and lowered her eyes again. This time they were filled with a joyous sparkle that I hadn't seen in her before.

"Then, when the time was right, I killed him." She said.

When I had come into the room, I had detected guilt on her face but now, as she talked about murdering him, she showed no signs of remorse at all. She actually looked happy. In spite of myself, I was pleased with her. I knew the lengths I would go to in order protect my daughter and if that failed, I didn't think there would be any limits to my revenge on anyone I found to be responsible.

I understood what she had done, and she had prevented me from having to do it. I was proud of her.

She explained to me that she had a fleeting moment of guilt when she saw me and thought of my loss, but that it couldn't last because she did the right thing. She explained how she had heard Malachi, Javari and me talking in the house about how I would be Chi if anything happened to Abram.

It sounded funny hearing the word Chi escape from her mouth with her smooth English accent.

She had put her faith in me to be a better person than my husband and to do the right thing by her people.

Malachi picked up her story from there. "I found these pills when I was searching her room," he explained. "These pills correlate with the toxin reports found in his bloodstream. So I came here and asked her to explain herself. She told me that she had crept into your room, Atarah. She had crept in whilst you had both slept, and silently dripped the crushed pills into his mouth. Just one would have killed him. She gave him four!"

Her nose had been dripping with blood as we had entered the room and now the flow had ceased and dried blood caked to her face, reddish brown and flaky. There was a black bruise forming rapidly round her eye. She suddenly reminded me a lot of her daughter.

Malachi put a black sack over her head.

"She knows a lot!" He said, "We are lucky she has kept it to herself."

We all looked at each other.

"I think we could all use some time to process this information." I told them. "Let's meet back here in ten minutes with some plans."

By the time we returned, Amelia had been killed. A laser assault pen had been used; it had drawn across her chest and her body lay in two halves in front of us, blood slowly congealing as it seeped out across the floorboards.

Chapter Twenty One – Another Confession

Seeing her there dead, I wondered who would initiate plans for her funeral. It was a strange thing to think about but here I was, her only friend in the world, if I could be described as that, and I couldn't do it because she had killed my husband. No matter how pleased I felt about that, I needed to keep up appearances.

I thought back to how I had done just that at Abram's funeral. I had worn a beautiful pink gown that I had commissioned from Shallimi. She had created my wedding dress and it seemed somehow fitting that she would create my mourning attire too. This was much more conservative than my wedding dress. As was custom, every inch of my body was covered. I wore a thin, dusty pink lace veil over my face. The dress itself was tight fitting and slender. It fell to the floor, highlighting my frame. It shimmered with tiny sequined jewels to remind everyone that Abram was in a better place now- he took his seat amongst the stars with the deity who created us.

Everyone in attendance formed a large circle- a ring of varying shades of pink: the colour of respect in Holiterian culture. The circle was huge but this wasn't on account of Abram's popularity. Just like me, half of his mourners were there out of a sense of propriety and decorum.

Abram's body lay, in uniform, on a large square of pink cloth. Myself and the three highest-ranking women from the village walked slowly towards him. The women wiped his face and feet with water to cleanse him. Once this ritual was complete we each took hold of one of the four corners of the cloth and gently wrapped his cold, hard body.

We turned our backs and chanted the song that I had sung when I first arrived on this planet. The circle was so large we had to chant it three times as we moved slowly back to our places within it.

Josiah, Samson, Javari and Malachi then moved to take their places by his side. Each carried with them a torch, which they lit from a small flame burning just a few metres from Abram's resting place. Everyone in the circle began to hum the sombre tune of the burning. As the men got closer to him, the humming decreased in volume and pace. When they were standing next to him they raised their arms together and silence fell amongst us.

They slowly lowered their arms and set fire to the pink cloth. We watched together, holding hands, as the flames began to grow. They twisted around the lifeless body taking on a deeper intensity as they did. The embers of his body began to glow red. Blue arms of fire reached upwards to heaven.

A thick black smoke began to rise. It took Abram's spirit to its resting place in the sky.

As his wife, I was considered chief mourner. It was therefore my place to decide when the circle should break and the congregation move away. I watched for as long as I could bear and then broke the circle. I turned and walked back towards the farm. The crowd followed me.

Only Mikea stayed. He had been tasked with the disposal of the ashes and any parts that remained.

It seemed so unfair that this monster, who had taken millions of lives and condemned thousands to suffer a cruel and tortured fate, was honoured with ceremony and respect. This beautiful human woman who had acted with bravery and strength would be honoured with nothing. No friends, no family, no ceremony.

It took me a moment to notice that Malachi was already there in the room, sat on Amelia's bed looking at her body. I had been too engrossed in my thoughts to notice.

He must have killed her within a matter of moments after Javari and I had left. Javari walked in shortly after the pieces had slotted together in my mind.

"I am sorry but I had to take the matter into my own hands. I didn't feel there was any other option. I didn't want you to have to make this decision because I know you had a good relationship with her." Malachi told me.

"Still," Javari argued, "It should have been her decision. She will be Chi after all!"

"Let's not fall about arguing with each other just yet. We need to deal with the task here first!" I told them both and they quickly settled down. "What's done is done. Now I think maybe you need to explain where you see us proceeding from here, Malachi."

His reasoning was flawless. There are some truths that just need to be kept a secret. He couldn't have ever rested knowing that Amelia was alive because her knowledge of Abram's involvement in the detonation of Earth's nuclear weapons would have crumbled the entire foundation on which we could build.

He knew life would work better here together if we could find a way to get along. We would be in for a lifetime of struggle and unrest if we did not find a mutually agreeable reason for us both to inhabit this land and work upon it in peace and harmony.

Our doctors are far superior to the ones on Earth so he explained how we could easily put people in place at the birthing suites to store the placentas after the births of children. They could sign a non-disclosure contract and nobody outside of the immediate medical circle would know that we were stealing antibodies from our patients. Clearly it would be more beneficial to us if humans did not realise that we needed them to survive. He had clearly given this a lot of thought in the short amount of time he had been here with Amelia.

"Atarah, in my mind, you could be Chi and we could all live alongside each other under your successful leadership."

I liked the sound of that.

Then Javari told me something I hadn't considered. If we leave this planet and they have any reason at all to hate us, then we will forever live in fear, wherever we go (our home planet or another) that the humans will want to hunt us down and declare war; particularly as their technology improves. It is no way to live when you are in constant fear from enemies.

I forgot sometimes just how amazing Javari was at his job.

There had been a lot of new information to process that day. By the end of it I had decided that I needed to focus on improving Earth, as the Holiterians here had mistakenly believed Abram had. I needed to put my faith in to this project in order to run this planet successfully.

I spoke to Malachi, who agreed that I was right; running one planet would be much simpler than running two. He was sure I could sever many of my ties to home and relinquish the control back to the Government of the People and that we could keep the Holiterian government in our favour and allegiance too. He put the cogs into motion for me and I began to plan for a way forward from there.

Chapter Twenty Two – The Art of Sophistry

On the day of my ceremony, I conducted a tour of my territories. I was driven through the compound, I drove through the villages that my own people had set up and I saw it all. People lined the streets to wave to me. The humans in their compounds were less enthusiastic but I was confident that I could change this in time.

My speech was given from the farmhouse at the end of the day. Every person was ordered to watch it. It was broadcast on a large hologram display in the compound and in the home of every other person here.

"My fellow men, women and children here on Earth- welcome! Today we shall all unite. We shall do this peacefully and for this, I thank you. I know you, like me, understand the need for change. Abram did things that none of us is proud of. Humans have been abused here at his hands and our men have been ordered to do things they deplored.

I have a vision of a better world. It is a world in which we live together peacefully, a world in which we are not rich because we have trodden on humans but because we have worked hard and deserve to be here. In my vision for the future there is no us and humans. We are all to be united under the title Earthers and I will lead you well to ensure that this land is a place of happiness for everyone.

Throughout Earth's history, revolutions have taken place. Some revolutions have been bloody, yet I hope that we have come far enough to make the necessary changes without the drawing of blood.

I hope this because I believe we have come far enough through civilisation to first use our voices as our swords.

As I am sure the native Earthers will admit, they did not run this planet as well as they should. They showed it little respect. Their politicians and leaders ended up annihilating the entire planet and almost killing its entire population in the name of nuclear warfare. Global warming was at an all time high and causing massive strains on the environment. Without intervention, the planet would have self-destructed anyway.

The native Earthers need us and our technology to rid their land of the radioactive poison. We can offer them our services to purge vast areas of land, as we have done on the compounds, to ensure their continued survival.

I offer my own services to preside over this land whilst it is re-established. I will continue with this duty until such a time as we are properly reformed and then I promise to ensure fair and honest elections of a Council of the People.

Once the Council of the People is working for your benefit, I will then step back and continue to pursue my own projects- I am, after all, a mother at heart.

I wish to lead us, the people, to the better world of which we all dream.

To those of you still who would consider opposing me and the progress that I represent, I ask you this- are you prepared to die in a broken world and wipe your species out with you?

I am here because I love our planet. I love our home. I love each of you.

Humans didn't have it right, Abram didn't have it right. The reason for this was because they were both looking out only for themselves. I offer an alternative. I offer to look out for everyone's interests. Earthers everywhere, I pray that you will unite under my guidance. "

I knew my speech was reminiscent of Abram's first speech to the people at the rally to the point of plagiarism. I knew his words would motivate and inspire everyone more than anything I could come up with because he had a way of convincing everyone to his way of thinking. I just hoped that I was some way towards exuding the charisma that accompanied his words too.

Javari came up to me and put his arm around me. "That was wonderful," he said. "And what's more wonderful is the fact that we no longer need to hide our relationship. We can be together properly and rule together."

He thrust his hand into his pocket and pulled out a small box.

"Javari, what are you doing?" I asked beginning to panic.

"I want to ask you if you will be my wife?" He asked with a voice alive with joy. "We finally have everything we wanted and can be together as a family."

Suddenly I saw everything I had worked for unravelling before my eyes. If people knew Javari and I were together, we would be open to accusations that might undermine my authority. Being a woman in power brought with it a lot of pressure. It was essential that I maintained a stance of infallibility. There should be no dirt on me, no gossip, nothing but good grace and standing.

Javari was stood there before me, wanting to play happy families. He wanted me to confess to the world that Esmella was his daughter. The scandal that would accompany that would be immense.

I had a short amount of time to ascertain what it was that I wanted here. Javari was offering me true love but at the expense of my newly found power. Malachi had made me Chi and that route, if played correctly, offered me power and security and wealth.

I truly did love Javari. Sometimes love isn't enough.

"I would love to be your wife!"

A sanguine joy spread across his face and he leaned in to kiss me. I put my arms around him and pulled him in closer to me.

His face contorted as he pulled back from me and shock filled his eyes. I had hoped he wouldn't have had time for the realisation to dawn on him. I had wanted to avoid seeing that betrayed, pained look in his eyes.

His hand dropped down to his stomach and clutched at the gaping wound where I had stabbed him. Warm, sticky blood oozed between his fingers and he lurched forward to grasp at me. I swiftly moved backwards and let him fall to the floor.

I leant down and kissed his forehead. It tasted salty and felt cold and clammy. The life was leaving his body.

"I am truly sorry." I whispered in his ear, "I love you, Javari."

I wept for a long time before I was collected enough to return to Malachi. He told me he would dispose of the body for me and no questions would be asked of me. He was going to put the body in the compound, as we had discussed, and a human would be blamed for the murder.

When Malachi had told me I would have to kill Javari to maintain my power, I had thought he was crazy. I didn't think I had it in me to kill the man I loved more than anyone else in the world. Malachi had given me the knife. He had given me the plot. He had given me the position of Chi. There was nothing we couldn't do working together.

It is interesting how, even with the constraints of a society that keeps women down, I have always found a way to get what I have wanted. Unfortunately, sometimes that means crushing those you love.

With Malachi behind me, there was nothing I couldn't do. He was a father figure and source of guidance for me. Together, we went on to set up the compound to keep the humans under our control whilst ensuring they had a better way of life.

I had become a queen.

Part Two

Death

*

Dearest Esmella,

Atarah was right my darling. You do have a right to know the truth about your mother. I cannot simply let you read this document that I have found and leave you to bear the burden of it though.

You must know how I came to possess it, what I have done with it and why.

Unlike your mother, I am not writing this just for the history books, I am writing this for you. I will tell my whole story because it is time that you knew every side of me and I have kept it a secret for too long. What follows is yours and I am writing it to you alone.

I want you to know what life was like living under your mother's rule. I want you to know why I have done the things I have done.

You are a better woman than your mother and I hope that, without her clipping your wings, you will be able to fly.

What you choose to do with me at the end of this is entirely up to you. I trust you to behave with integrity and morality and do whatever you feel to be right.

Yours always,

José x

Chapter One – Life in a Compound

Living under Holiterian dictatorship is hell for us. I am the bottom of the pile; Holiterians are above Humans. Females are above Males. I, as a human male, am underneath them all and I feel the weight of them every day.

I was born into this so have never known anything different, but people still speak of a better life and how wonderful things used to be. It is hard for me to imagine.

I sometimes wonder if they remembered things as they were or if they have romanticised them over time. The world they had before sounded wonderful but I think anything would be compared to what we live in now.

They talk of a time of lazy afternoons, sitting watching entertainment on boxes called televisions which digitally transmitted moving images of people acting out stories. I suppose these are a little like the holographic boxes we have now. They reminisce about holidays; visits abroad, weekends by the sea, city breaks, cruises, stunning architecture.

My parents have described to me in glorious detail their visit to Prague when they first started dating. Prague was a small city in the Czech Republic. They recalled with laughter the walk up what my mother assured me was 'a million steep steps' up to the castle. My Dad joked that she had moaned all the way to the top that they should have taken the tram. He was walking behind her as they ascended, pretending to push her to keep her moving but she was out of breath and fed up with looking up at a never-ending set of gravelled steps so she stopped and turned around. With a look of absolute awe, she spun my father around too and together, hand in hand, they looked out in the glorious sunshine over a beautiful city. Spires shaped the skyline and they both posed for a 'selfie' with that fabulous backdrop behind them.

They had taken a hundred photographs that weekend, self images like the one with the scenic views, and images of the places they saw. All those images were lost now and they had to keep telling the stories to keep them alive in their memories.

By night, they explained, the city had become even more stunning. They had taken a jazz boat cruise down the river and drank and danced whilst the charming city had been lit up around them. Gothic architecture, illuminated in the night, rose above them. The details had begun to fade in their minds but they both recalled the astounding beauty of it.

And the cobbled streets; they always came back to the quaint maze of cobbled streets they had followed around the Old Town and a charming little tea room they had stumbled upon. They had sat on cushions around a low table and been served an array of different types of tea in little china pots.

They speak of regret at how they had taken their freedom for granted and wasted so much of the free time they had been blessed with.

It made me sad to think that I would never experience a holiday or get to see the beautiful landmarks my parents described. I imagine they are all long gone now.

We live every day within the confines of the compound. The Councillors keep us living under the scrutiny of their tyranny. They are as power hungry as your mother, Chi Atarah.

We are on a 6pm curfew. Every day at this time, the siren sounds out across the whole compound. The few people who were left out on the streets scurry quickly back to their homes. They are like little mice, scuttling into their holes. We are all like vermin to the Holiterians. Then, shortly after the sirens stop, the soldiers march in pairs down the streets, prowling for prey to toy with. Curtains slide shut as they pass and voices hush in the homes as they wait for the sound of the footsteps to pass.

My father speaks to me sometimes of the week that the curfew came into place; outrage had spread through us like wildfire. Men were furious. Not only did they keep us on this compound, cooped up like animals in a zoo, but now they were going to restrict us even further.

A group who called themselves The Fury had taken to the streets the first night. They were fearless and broken and felt there was nothing left to lose. They put pillow cases over their heads as it was the closest thing they could find to a mask to disguise their individuality.

They left their homes on the strike of six. They bore placards their wives had made. Their anonymity made them brave and they howled like wolves as they ran through the streets waving their signs of defiance. Worried mothers and wives watched them through the windows.

They had become caught up in the moment and ended up smashing windows of shops as they ravaged the village attempting to destroy everything that was inflicted on them by their Holiterian leaders. Their howling turned to wild hysterical laughter. It was the first taste of freedom they had experienced since our hell had begun. It had been a long time since they had exercised any freewill and they were embracing it. A group mentality spread through them and they collectively became destructive.

My mother spoke of how the sounds of laughter and howling drew others out into the streets; The Fury were growing in numbers and they rolled through the streets, drawing in more and more people as they went. Before long every man, woman and child was out there, running amok. There is something in human nature that I have seen in yours too, a desire to fight and to be a part of something. The Fury wasn't an exclusive group- everyone could join and they all wanted to because they were all tired of being the victims.

They crowded around the houses of the councillors. They stamped their feet and clapped their hands and whistled an eerie tune they had been composing and learning as they worked on the fields during the day. It quickly caught on and soon everyone was joining in together. It filled the night air.

The Holiterians had anticipated their move. My father told me that he never knew whether they had made a lucky guess or whether they had an informant working on the inside, but either way, they were ready for us.

Guards appeared at the windows holding laser assault pens. Every single one of them had been in the hospitals and knew the capabilities of those weapons. They stopped in their tracks. The door opened. Chi Atarah stood there.

"We've let you have your fun." She glanced around at the damage we had created, "It seems you will have a lot of work tomorrow because I expect all of this" she looked down with disdain, "to be fixed."

Anger filled the hearts of every person there. They realised she had let them riot simply to give them more work to do. They hated her beyond all measure.

"You are here because you have to be; the world outside of this compound would kill you. Are you so stupid and self-destructive that you can't see the good we have done for you?"

This story was told again and again amongst our people. It still is. Your mother was villainised. We needed a common enemy to unite us. Whether she was helping us or holding us captive, she was at the head of the people who had come to our planet and made themselves our superiors. For this reason, I fear for you in the position you now find yourself.

The second night after the curfew was enacted, The Fury comprised of just three men. They never returned home and The Fury disbanded.

Life isn't easy. We have to get up with the sun every morning irrespective of the weather. We need to produce all the food that we eat which means we have had to learn long forgotten skills of working the land. We sow seeds and reap the harvests. The machinery our people used to use, that my parents told me about, was never given to us. And not only do we have to support and feed ourselves and our families, we have to produce food to support the Holiterians too.

I was four years old the first time I went to work in the fields. I was sent out with my father. Even though he tried to shield me from it as much as he could, it was back-breaking work.

The ground was barren and hard. I had to dig into it using a spade almost as tall as I was. I thrust it down into the soil and nothing happened. I watched the other men and boys effortlessly glide the metal through the earth. Sweat glistened on their brows and arms but they made it look easy.

I wanted more than anything to make my mother proud of me. I knew that she would be sad to think of me out here hurt or in pain, so I picked the spade back up and brought it down again with all the force I could muster. Slowly the soil had begun to part and angry, red blisters had formed on the side of my hand.

When I had returned home that evening my mother had kissed those painful, fluid-filled pockets. I had flinched each time her lips came into contract with my raw, stinging flesh and smiled as sweetly as I could as her eyes had filled with tears. My father had told me that I needed to be strong for her.

The second day was worse. I went to work with my delicate brown skin throbbing from the day before. Just picking up my spade was excruciating. I wanted so much to cry and run to my dad but it wasn't possible. I had to be strong, so I was, and eventually my blisters became calluses.

Now I am strong and muscular but I am lucky; not all the men are fed as I am. I see the old men in our society and the damage that the years of labour has done to them. I weep for my future. There is no care system in place for us when we can no longer work.

There is a sense of community within our compound. Fierce friendships form in the face of adversity. We do, however, have problems with humans being recruited to be on the side of the Councillors. They walk among us but are the eyes and ears of the Holiterian Police Force (The HPF). They ensure our behaviour is in line with Holiterian rules and they prevent the possibility of planning a coup.

Not that we could, if we wanted to. Your mother has ensured that we cannot leave the compound due to the radiation levels; I defy you to tell me that it wouldn't have been possible for her to clear up a greater area with her technology should she have wished.

I am often viewed with an air of suspicion too. As you know, I was chosen to work in your household. I came to you when I was just ten years old. I had already been working for years out on the fields. Now I was to do this just two days a week; the other five I was picked up from the compound in a large, radiation-proof armoured vehicle. When a human has such regular, close contact with the Holiterians, it is hard to blame others for doubting their allegiance.

I remember vividly the first time I was brought to your home. I was getting ready to go to the field when an inspection was called. Sirens hollered. People began rushing out of their homes to take their position in a parade. We all lined up, young and old together. It wasn't an uncommon occurrence so we all got into position without too much worry. The HPF strode past us with an authoritarian gait.

That day was slightly different though. The soldiers were there too. A tall solider, with dull silver skin and bright blue hair strutted confidently along, eyeing each of us carefully before moving on to the next.

As he got to me, he nodded and pulled me out of line. "You will come with me, boy," he commanded.

I felt panic ravage me. I turned to look at my mum and dad for guidance. Their faces had turned the colour of porcelain and dread filled their big, brown eyes.

"Please, sir," my mother began, "not my son!"

There were stories of the HPF taking people from the streets. It wasn't an entirely uncommon occurrence. When people went missing, there were often reports of them having been seen bundled away previously. The HPF drives large black vehicles that hover off the ground. I sometimes wonder if they think they are too good to touch the ground on which we humans walk. They are arrogant enough to think it, I am sure. The vehicles have black mirrored windows. I suppose from the inside they must be able to see out, but if we look at them, all we can see is a blackened reflection of ourselves.

Apparently, before the Holiterian rule if someone committed a crime, they were given a trial. This was an opportunity for them to prove their innocence, or for a prosecutor to prove their guilt. Either way, all the facts were given and accounted for.

Now, if someone was accused of breaking a Holiterian rule, the blackened craft hovers alongside them, two men dressed in either the green HPF uniform, or occasionally the red uniform of the soldiers, jump out, grab them and throw them into the vehicle before zooming away. They are never seen again.

There is no closure for families because we never know what has happened. They could be in a prison, or dead. There is no way to find out. The older women and men in our compound had been in the original prisons and they talk of the torture that took place there and the medical experiments. Rumours are rife that this may still be happening.

I imagine all this was running through my mother's mind when she reached forward to pull me back into the line again. I felt her warm hand lock onto my hand and I clenched her tightly. The solider, looming over me in his blood-red uniform, seized my other hand simultaneously and pulled- hard. I thought I might split in two but my mother loved me too much to let that happen and she let me go.

Every bone in my body wanted to cry and run to her; I was her little fighter and I knew I couldn't let this guard kill me in front of her. It would devastate her. I looked bravely into her eyes with all the valour a ten year old boy could contain and told her that I would be alright.

I choked back the tears as he led me to the compound gates. I was terrified of stepping outside for fear of the radiation killing me but there was a bulky black vehicle there waiting and the guard told me to get in and I would be fine. I had nothing to do but trust him.

When I left that morning, I didn't know if I was ever going to see my parents again. It is hard to explain now just how petrified and distressed I was.

I was alone in the back of the huge black van. It wasn't a hover vehicle; it was a modified human vehicle. I rattled around in the back as we sped round corners and over bumps. By the time it stopped my bravado and courage had dissolved and I was a dishevelled, weeping, snotty mess of a child.

The soldiers came to the back and opened the door.

"Stop snivelling, child. You are about to meet the Chi and the last thing she wants in her home is a weak, blubbering wimp."

I resented him speaking to me like that. I wiped my eyes and resolved to be a man. I thought of my father and pretended to be just like him. I thought of my mother and drew as much strength as I could from her.

I was going to meet the Chi. That woman had us living in purgatory and I wasn't going to give her the satisfaction of grovelling to her. I decided to go to her and accept willingly whatever fate became me. I may only have been ten years old but my childhood had been stolen from me at the age of four.

I walked between the soldiers with my head held high. Everything went past me in a blur. My legs shook and it took all my concentration to still them. My mind raced. I was brought before her- the Chi, your mother.

She was such a beautiful woman that for a moment I forgot how much I hated her. Her hair fell softly around her shoulders. I knew, even at that young age, I was supposed to view silver and cornflower shades of skin with hatred and loathing. I was supposed to be repulsed by hair with a metallic shine of cobalt blues. But her appearance and presence had a potency that was difficult to ignore.

I bowed before her. Then I thought of everyone back on the compound and felt embarrassed for the betrayal to my own people. I stood up hastily.

"Welcome," she said. Her voice was almost kind. It is funny how appearances can be deceptive. "You are probably wondering why I have brought you here."

I nodded, "Yes Ma'am."

"I want a boy to work here for five days of your human week. The other two you can work back on your compound. I am not so heartless as to keep an infant from its mother."

"Thank you, Ma'am." Relief flooded my body. I was going to see my parents again.

"You will be completing general chores around my building. Boys are much more trustworthy than men." She spoke like someone who had been crossed by a human before. I think she believed she would be safer with me because of the naivety of my youth. Perhaps she thought it would be easier to brainwash me to her own way of thinking and to corrupt me against my own kind. My biggest fear was that she would recruit me to be an HPF informant. I would rather die than betray my own.

I was never asked to report to anyone about anything though. I worked hard during the days, slept in the basement of the farm house during the evenings and was returned home at the weekends. I settled quickly into this routine.

My room on the farm is nicer than my one at home. On the compound, our house is filled with other people's photos and memories and tastes and has been stuck in a time warp since the explosions happened. Part of our house had been ransacked in looting that had taken place before we had all been captured and placed into hospitals and compounds, but we were one of the lucky ones and much of the furniture and artwork remained. My mother did the best she could with what was available to us.

There is a picture that hangs on my bedroom wall of a small boy looking up at a beautiful woman who is smiling down at him. He is probably only two or three and is full of promise and joy. He is holding a small, caramel coloured stuffed rabbit toy by its ear. My mother wanted to get rid of it when we were located there. It was my father who suggested we keep it. We had no photos of our own and he wanted something to make the house we were imprisoned in feel like a home. As I grew up it quickly became one of my favourite images. It was something real I could see that accompanied the stories people shared of the Old World.

But it also made me sad. Everything about our home reminded my parents of a happy time and gave them hope of a time to come but it didn't have the same meaning to me. Their world was one I never had the opportunity to experience. For me it was a carefully preserved history book that I enjoyed flicking through, but all the people were dead and gone. The small boy in the photo in my room had his life ripped tragically away from him. As I got older, I found it increasingly morbid.

On the farm, everything was fresh and shiny. My room is lit with an artificial light as there are no windows in the basement. It is the most natural, beautiful light though. It is better than having a window because it only ever shows me glorious, happy sunshine.

I don't come back at the end of the day exhausted from working on the fields, only to collapse onto a bed surrounded by reminders of how my life could have been. I come back, simply tired, and sink onto a comfy mattress on the floor and stare at blank walls that I can write all over with my own hopes and dreams and decoration.

At night, when I switch off the lights, I am plunged into a perfect darkness. There are no bright, sweeping HPF lights blaring intermittently through my window. I love the complete blackness; it shuts off all my senses and allows me to forget everything and just be me.

Don't misunderstand though; I love going home to my parents. I just found myself quite quickly liking being with you too.

Chapter Two - Esmella

The first weekend I came home my mother and father wept for joy. They didn't know if I would be returned to them and had spent a week in agony, mourning for their lost son.

The same radiation proof van that had stolen me away was the one to return me. It was after dark and I had completed a hard day's work for Chi Atarah and hadn't realised that it was the day I would be taken home again. Joy filled my young heart when I realised and I ran to that van as quickly as I could. We bumped back along the roads the way we had come and the journey seemed to take forever, as journeys always do when you are so desperately anticipating the end point.

I was kicked out by the soldiers at the compound gates. It was after six and I had a special pass so that the HPF would allow me safe passage if they should see me. I wasn't seen.

I ran and ran through the dark streets. Ferocious shadows danced in alleyways and feral beasts seemed to howl in the distance. My heart thudded in my chest and my legs burnt as I continued to run. I arrived home panting and collapsed into the jubilant arms of my family.

After filling them in on the details of my week and my new job with the Chi, I went to bed and listened to the hushed tones of my parents' worried voices.

I hadn't met you during my first week.

The adults on the compound knew exactly who you were. It didn't take them long to see an opportunity and hatch a plan to find our way in.

Atarah was hideously out of control. As long as she was in power our lives would be hell. They discussed how by getting to you we might have options. You were next in line to inherit the throne. If you loved one of us, then you might be kinder to us than your mother. We know we had complete dependence on the Holiterians now. However, any weakness on your part would have the potential to give us the upper hand and resume power over our planet at such a time when the radiation levels made it permissible. This is the long term goal of every human here. In the shorter term, we dream of equality.

I realise that what I am saying now may hurt you. Also, though it is true that I initially befriended you for selfish reasons, my feelings for you are true and if you feel anything for me at all, you will keep reading.

I returned to your farm again on the Monday. I met the soldiers at the gate that time, got willingly into their van and bumped to the farm quite happily. I had quite enjoyed my first week there. Although I had a lot of chores to do, none were as backbreaking as working the fields. The food was better too. I was allowed to eat anything left over from the main tables and in comparison to what we have access to on the compound, it was exquisite.

And I had a mission.

For the first time, I had been invited into the hushed underground resistance meetings on our compound. For the whole weekend the discussions had centred on me and it seemed I had given them fresh hope. I was the first human taken to work there. There were stories of a maid who had once worked there but she had betrayed Atarah and had been put to death. Since then, humans were all confined to the compound, until now.

My mother chaired the meetings. People arrived under the cover of darkness through a series of underground tunnels using the old sewage systems which ran under our town.

It was a difficult time to arrange such things, especially with HPF spies masquerading among us. The women were in charge of the meetings but the men came too as they were invariably the brawn that carried out the plans that were conceived.

Sure enough, in spite of the dangers and a very real threat of espionage, at 8 o'clock on the dot, people began to arrive. Exhausted from their day on the fields, they came up, as they always do, through a hole drilled out in the basement.

I have ventured down there a few times. You have to trudge through a good few inches of sludge and slime even though it isn't used for sewage anymore. Moisture drips from the top and you find yourself getting splodges of rank smelling, green liquid sliding over your skin. There are a few surviving rats and insects down there too. Even now, if I am honest, it gives me the creeps walking around in it.

Once everyone had arrived for the meeting at our house that night, Edith, a scraggy woman with long, blonde, matted hair and stone cold blue eyes that could turn your heart to ice in seconds, came over to me and eyed me suspiciously. She then lifted her bony finger and jabbed me on my cheek. In spite of myself, I winced from the pain.

"Can he be trusted?" She asked accusingly, "after all, he is working for them now!"

It was the first time anyone had questioned my integrity and I felt the sting of her words. I had expected everyone to jump to my defence; these were my neighbours and friends. These people had known me my whole life. Everyone just looked at me in anticipation. I felt tears prick in my eyes and I swallowed back a rock of emotion that had risen itself into my throat.

It was my mother that jumped to my defence.

"How dare you," she scowled. "That's my son. He's just ten years old but he knows what is right and what is wrong. He may be a child but he's honest and loyal and if you dare lay a finger on him again you'll have me to deal with!"

Even now I tower over her I still shrink back to a child when she reprimands me. My mother can be fierce. She is a good woman though and she deserves more than the life she has.

Edith recoiled at my mother's chastisement too and with that, the meeting was called to order. It was hard for me to keep up with the pace of the conversation at just the age of ten; I knew nothing of politics really. I just knew that life was hard. It was once everybody else had left that my parents explained what I had to do.

My target was to find you. You were just eight years old at the time. My people hoped that Holiterians were not inherently evil and that I might be able to sway you to our cause before it was too late. I suppose your mother thought the same of me at my young age too. Once I had found you I had to make you care about me. How to do that baffled me.

I had been told that there was an element of risk involved. If Chi Atarah discovered our friendship it could mean I would be returned to the compound and never allowed to return to the farm. The better alternative was that, if your mother realised you cared for me, you might be able to convince her that I should be allowed to stay and work for you.

Whatever the outcome, it was believed that a friendship between us would put humans in a better light in the eyes of the heir to the throne and therefore secure our future after the demise of your mother.

So that is how I came to be at the farm the second week, trying to ascertain who was the daughter to the Chi and how on earth I might find a way to meet her.

It turned out you were easier to find than I thought. The second night of that week, your mother was throwing a party. My job was to serve drinks and, I suppose, be something of a spectacle for the Holiterians to look at during their meal.

The guests were flowing in steadily and mingling in the garden. There were men in red uniforms with navy belts around their waists with different coloured stitching on. I quickly discovered that more stitching equated to a higher ranking. Each man arrived in the company of a glamorously dressed woman. Their hair, in varying shades of silver and blues, all hung in soft curls around their faces. This was obviously the style of the time because now you tend to wear your hair pulled back off your faces much more.

I loved you with soft silver ringlets falling down your shoulders. It was the longest, most beautiful hair I had ever seen.

And there I stood. One of the Holiterian men also serving that night had scrubbed me up as best he could, but I was still thin and scraggy. I was malnourished and in the midst of youth. My muscles had not yet developed as they have now. It was easy to see why you all thought yourself so much better than us when you could dress in your finery and look at me as I was.

I had a job to do and it wasn't easy. Trays balanced with fifteen glasses, filled with liquid, were placed precariously on my hands. I wobbled. I was threatened with a beating if I spilled any. I walked in constant fear. I handed out all my glasses and went back to the kitchens to be handed more. And everyone there wanted to take the time to stop me and look down on me and some asked me questions. I just felt awkward and embarrassed. I desperately wanted to focus on my glasses but I also knew it was my job to be pleasant to the guests.

I wondered what my parents would think of me making polite conversation with the hated Holiterians. I felt guilty being polite to them but I knew I had to be to achieve my mission- to cultivate our friendship. I also knew that, if I didn't follow my orders correctly, I would be subject to the hands of these violent and abusive people. They seemed friendly enough but I think they were only kind to me then because I was just a child and, for the women, the closest they had ever come to seeing a human in the flesh.

I was relieved when the guests were called through to dinner. At least for that part of the evening they were all sat down and too busy discussing political affairs and the chef's handiwork to notice me struggling to fill up their glasses from a bottle the size of my torso.

Once the meal was finished I began to relax. There was a bar open in the ballroom for drinks and I mistakenly thought that my role might be over. I am so glad it wasn't.

Chi Atarah came barging into the kitchens and tension immediately raged through the staff. "You," she said looking at me. I panicked. "Everyone has taken quite an interest in you. You will be a darling and come and dance with my daughter, Esmella. It will be quite the spectacle to entertain everyone."

I wasn't really sure what I had to do as I had never danced before. We never had the time or the energy on the compound and any such display of merriment was sure to be shut down quickly by the HPF. Nonetheless, I stepped out into the hallway. I felt like some sort of animal being made to perform for the enjoyment of the crowd and I didn't feel good about being a 'spectacle'. Nonetheless, I was pleased that I would meet you.

There you were in the hallway. I had thought that your mother was beautiful but you were in another league entirely. Your skin was so pale silver you could almost have been white yet it shimmered in the light with the metallic hue that is native to your race. You were wearing a dusky pink dress that came to the floor and you swished it around you like a fairytale princess.

I was mesmerised by the sparkle and the way the light seemed to illuminate you. The belt of diamonds around your waist dazzled me. Your skin sparkled and your hair shone and the shimmer in your dress danced. I couldn't peel my eyes away.

You looked at me nervously when you saw me looking at you; I guessed you had never seen a human before. Then you gave me the biggest smile. You took my breath away. I knew immediately that you were good and I knew in my heart that I could never ever use you.

You led me out onto that dance floor like you were a little grown up and you knew exactly what to do. I clumsily followed your lead and the crowd made 'ooh' and 'ahh' noises and laughed at us. You played to the crowd because you knew that they loved you and I shied away from the attention because I knew they didn't value me or my life.

Back at the compound I told them that we had danced together. I wasn't the type to lie, especially not to my parents. I told them it seemed unlikely we would get to spend any more time together because you always had a body guard by your side. This I knew was only a half truth because by the end of that week, I had heard your mother complaining that you had given poor Clai the slip for the hundredth time and disappeared off on your own again.

This information was enough to make my parents ease up some of the pressure they had on me to manipulate you, and to encourage them to go back to looking for alternative plans.

Chapter Three – A Forbidden Friendship

You always told me you didn't have anybody to play with; there were no children on the farm, you were never permitted into the village as your mother was too worried about your safety and the adults on the farm were too busy carrying out your mother's orders. You were bored and lonely.

You had enjoyed dancing with me that night.

About a week later, after losing poor Clai once again, you came to find me as I was sat in the dining room polishing cutlery and attempting to get all the smear marks off the beautiful and expensive glassware. You came in, sat down next to me and began to help.

Neither of us said a word the whole time you were sat there. I kept thinking of things I should say but then I would look at you and they would slip away again. You didn't look as if you needed words. I was shocked at your brazen and seemingly bizarre behaviour. You were such a free-spirit that I was envious of you but to be honest, I was grateful of the company.

The second time you disappeared and turned up where I was working, I plucked up the courage to introduce myself.

"Hi, I'm José."

"Esmella," you said and gave me another wicked grin like the smile before we had danced.

You asked me, as you have done many times since, about life in the compound. I never wanted to talk to you about it. You were so pure and innocent that I didn't want you to be sullied with the information of what your mother was doing. Of course, now you are going to find out anyway, I think it is only fair that I tell you my truth too.

We opted instead to talk about our dreams for the future. I told you I dreamed of a day when I can fall in love like my parents and be out after six and eat as much food as I need. You told me about your dreams of freedom too; you wanted to be free of bodyguards and your mother's constraints. You thought we had a lot in common because we both felt like we were being held captive. In a way we were but I am glad that you never worked out the differences between us. You are a remarkable person and you deserved to keep your childhood preserved for as long as possible. I resented every Holiterian that I met but you were different.

I began to look forward to our little meetings. It was nice to have a friend I could talk to. We would ask each other silly questions like "would you rather have an arm cut off or a leg cut off?" and would sit and deliberate our answers for ages before falling into a fit of giggles.

One of my favourite memories was the drizzly, grey day when you found me outside, in the barn. I had been sent out to bang off the thick mud that had crusted onto the resident soldiers' boots and polish them all up. It was a messy task so I had headed outside to do it. I had all the boots lined up. Cracked mud was sprinkled all over the floor and I was just contemplating sweeping that up whilst the polish dried, when you walked in. You were soaking wet and your hair dripped around your face.

"I wouldn't go out there. The rain is hammering down!" you beamed.

I looked at you and we both giggled. "You're going to be in big trouble again!"

"Better to be in trouble than unnoticed," you said.

I remember it vividly because I couldn't imagine how anyone could ever not notice you. Even then I thought you were vibrant, witty and stunning.

"Hide-and-seek?" You asked.

I didn't know what that was because playing was a new concept to me. You had to explain the rules to me before we could begin. You hid first and I counted. I knew where you were the moment I turned around but even though I was unfamiliar with the game, I realised I needed to humour you. So I looked around the barn for a good couple of minutes before I crept up behind you and made you jump out of your skin as I put my hands on your back and shouted 'boo!'

We both collapsed into a heap on the floor and stayed there, chatting for ages until I noticed the sun was breaking through again.

"We better get back before someone starts looking for one of us," I said, slightly worried.

"I guess so," you conceded before throwing your arms around me haphazardly and squeezing me tightly goodbye.

You were the first person who wasn't my mother or my father to ever hug me and it took me by surprise. I suddenly realised that you were actually my friend and I smiled.

On a more sombre note, I also remember the day we were sat in the library and you were helping me to stuff invitations to a formal event your mother was throwing into envelopes. Then Clai came in.

"What the hell is going on in here?" he yelled. He marched over to me, picked me up by one of my ears and pulled me towards the door. You cried out for him to leave me alone and hung onto his arm but he was no match for either of us. He shook you off onto the floor and hauled me outside.

I wasn't sure what was going to happen but then I saw his fist coming towards my face; I felt an intense pain as it made contact with me and my brain shook around in my skull. The world went black.

When I came around I had been tied to a tree in the middle of the garden. My head was buzzing and, as I tried to lift it, a pain seared down through my neck. My arms were tied tightly and, as I wiggled my fingers, pins and needles shot through them. It was cold outside and I had no shoes on. My toes felt numb and I could see they were beginning to look blue. The pain of the cold biting into my feet was nothing compared to the agonising throbbing in my ribcage.

I had no idea how long I had been tied there for. I tried to look up at the house but my vision was blurred and my eyeballs hurt in their sockets. The pain was so awful that I passed out again.

When I woke up it was raining. I was sodden and aching and hungry. The sun had begun to go down in the sky and the evening was drawing in. I was becoming increasingly afraid that I might be left there all night.

Then I heard the gentle whirl of a hover vehicle coming up the drive. It was your mother. I feared a fresh batch of torture was coming my way as she got out of her vehicle and sauntered over to me whilst one of her soldiers stood behind her with a large parasol over her head. The heels of her shoes were sinking into the muddy ground yet somehow she still managed to maintain her poise and grace.

"What on earth are you doing out here?" She asked. The way she asked made it seem like she thought I had made a choice to hang out there on the tree.

"Punishment, Ma'am," I told her and winced as a cut on my lip tore itself open and I realised how dry my throat was. In spite of my promise to myself on arriving at the farm that I would always be a man, I felt tears well in my eyes. I was tired, I was frightened and I was in pain. I decided that just this one I could forgive myself a moment's weakness and I let out a quiet sob as tears ran down my young face.

"And what, may I ask, was your crime?" She said seemingly hardened and oblivious to my plight.

I felt like she was toying with me. I feared she already knew I had been talking to her daughter and was just going to make me say it so that she could hurt me for it all over again.

"I.. I was.. er."

"Spit it out, child!" She demanded.

"I was working in the library. Esmella came in and we were talking and she was helping me work. I know I shouldn't have let her come in and I know it should have been me working and-"

"For goodness sake, breathe!" She said then turned to the soldier and went on, "Get this boy down from here. He is really of no use to me if he is dead and I can't be doing with the hassle of training a new one!"

Like that, it was over. You later told me that you spent the whole afternoon looking out of your window at me whilst Clai held his post outside your bedroom door. You looked out at me and cried for my release. When you saw your mother come in you went downstairs and threw yourself at her feet and told her how it wasn't my fault and how awfully unfair it all was. She stroked your hair and hugged you but to your surprise she didn't reproach Clai for his harsh punishments.

When I went home that weekend my mother was furious at the state of me. I couldn't bring myself to tell her the whole truth because I didn't want her to know that I had been talking to you. She was too angry at the sight of my beaten and bruised body that she didn't care about listening to my story anyway. On the plus side, I think having a cause to fight for keeps my mother going and gives her a reason to never give up. She set off on a whole new war path with a renewed drive and fury.

When I came back to the farm, you snuck off to see me and cried at my feet when you saw my face. I had to walk away from you because I feared what they would do to me if they found us playing together and honestly, I didn't trust them with you either. You told me it would break your heart if we couldn't be friends. I told you that you would get over it. I should have told you that it was breaking my heart too. You were my first and only true friend.

Chapter Four – Love

We went too long without talking. We would still smile at each other covertly, in passing, when we were sure nobody was looking. I watched from afar as you grew, transforming into the beautiful woman that you are today.

It frustrated me to see you every day and not be able to talk to you openly or to continue the friendship we had shared. Being your friend had made my life easier for me. You had given me something to look forward to each week and a reason to think that life could be better and your people could show mine kindness.

The void you left was never filled.

Even though a wedge had been driven between us, I still looked forward to coming to work. You were the closest thing I had to a friend; you still are. I may not have been one of you but I felt more at home in your home than I did in my own on the compound. I had you to thank for that.

It was fairly early on when I began to view my weekend trips home with a sense of foreboding. Whilst I was always pleased to see my mother and father, I no longer fitted in there. I had changed since coming here and people could sense it.

As I worked out on the fields with the other men, I could feel their resentment towards me. I only had to do this for two days of the week whereas they were out there every day from dawn until dusk. I think they imagined me living a life of luxury in your household and to be fair, compared to their lives, I truly was. They thought of me as a spy.

They gave me the nickname 'pretty boy' and would often pile dirt where I should be digging or give me the spade that was broken. I was always last to be offered water when the weather was hot, if I were lucky enough to be offered it at all. And yet I thrived. I was well fed and rested all week on your farm. They deteriorated because this was their whole life, all day, every day. I can see their point; it was incredibly unfair for them.

When they originally learnt of my posting here I had given them hope. They thought I could befriend you to further their cause. I had failed them in that. I offered them no information that was of any use in ending the Holiterian regime. I was useless to them. And I think there was an aspect of jealousy to it as well. I can't blame them for their bitterness towards me and I have come to accept it. That doesn't mean that it doesn't hurt me.

And the thing that hurt the most was the look I got every time the HPF destroyed one of our plans or found the location of one of our secret meetings. Even though I have never snitched on one of my own, the look of disdain and hatred and betrayal always falls on my doorstep first.

At least on the farm I had you to look at.

As I went passed through my teenage years, I would begin to feel myself blush when we passed each other on the stairs. I would look at you and wish I could touch you. I would see you talking and get lost in the movements of your lips. I longed to kiss those lips.

It took me a while to realise that the innocent friendship we had built together had blossomed into a romantic love on my part. I saw no way for us to ever be together though. We were from different worlds with different coloured skins. I didn't see the colour difference but I knew everyone else did. You were a princess and I was your slave. It was hardly the making of a lifelong romance and I had to find a way to make peace with that.

I hadn't realised, until you clandestinely sent me a note, that you had felt the same about me. You asked me if I would permit you to meet me in my bedroom in the basement. You explained it was the only place I would be afforded any privacy and that nobody was likely to come looking for you. You told me you had watched me for a long time and that you thought you might be in love with me. You told me how you would understand if I decided it was too dangerous and not worth the risk but that you would arrive that evening and knock on the door three times, then wait three seconds and then knock again twice.

I waited in my room, filled to the brim with concern, panic, horror, worry and more than anything else, ecstatic joy. I felt my heart racing and my palms grew sweaty as I sat there. Every noise outside made me jump to attention. When you finally knocked on the door, I let you in without a moment's hesitation.

"Thank you for letting me in," you said.

"How could I not? How could I deny you anything?"

I had no idea how long I would have you in my room. I didn't know if someone might come and drag you from me any moment and I didn't want to waste a single moment when I could be telling you how I felt. I didn't know if you would be able to come back again.

You clearly felt that same sense of urgency because you jumped straight to the point.

"Do you mean that? Do you think you might love me too?"

"I know I do," I told you honestly.

"Even though it is difficult?" you asked with those huge, eyes looking up at me.

"Being with you for a few minutes would be better than never getting to be with you," I told you.

Then you leaned over to me and kissed me. I had never been kissed before and it felt awkward at first. I wasn't sure if I was doing it right. But you seemed so confident and you took the lead. So I let you. I followed your guidance and I began to relax. Kissing you felt right and I wondered how we had gone though our lives having never done it before. I wondered, now I had experienced it, how we were going to get through the rest of our lives if we might never get to do it again.

Your lips were so delicate and your mouth was warm and inviting. You slid your tongue forward and pushed it gently into mine and I had to pull away because I could feel myself becoming hard and I didn't want to embarrass you. I remember the inquisitive look you gave me as you asked, "did I do something wrong?" and I held you to me as tightly as I could. I wanted you to know you could never do anything wrong.

We lay down together on my bed and picked up our conversations exactly where we had put them down all those years before. It turned out our dreams were still similar and neither of us felt any closer to achieving them. Time fluttered past us and before we knew it, the clock in the hallway was chiming four o'clock. The household would be springing awake soon and you needed to get back to your room before they did.

Once you had left, I sat there for a long time wondering how it was possible that so much time had passed us by without a word and yet we were as comfortable and easy together as we had ever been. I thought about that wonderful kiss. It felt so unreal that I began to worry it might have imagined it; I feared that it might have just been an amazing dream. But my heart knew it was real.

We began to meet up more and more. The only place we could safely do that was in my room under the cover of darkness. I don't know how we survived on as little sleep as we did but at least two nights each week, you would sneak down into my room once everyone had gone to sleep. It helped that your bodyguards no longer slept directly outside your room, but it was still difficult and risky. We didn't care though.

As soon as you arrived, we would laugh together and right the wrongs of the world. We would both fantasise about a world in which humans and Holiterians lived side by side in unity; we dreamed of the world in which we could be together without judgement and hatred.

And our relationship moved forward physically too. I have to admit I had some trepidation about having sex with you. Not only was it my first time, I wasn't one hundred percent sure that our bodies would work together in that way. Admittedly pigmentation had proved to be the only major difference between our species, that and some facial contouring, but I didn't know if we were similar enough where it counted for us to be able to sleep together.

I had nothing to worry about. Other than how quickly it was all over for me the first time! You told me it was flattering and I thank you to this day for protecting my ego, but I know you felt a twinge of disappointment. It didn't take us long to work out the rhythm of each other's bodies though. Being with you feels so natural and so right. It doesn't matter that I am human and you are Holiterian. We are two people in love. Our conversation sparkles and our bodies work together and know each other intimately. How can that be wrong?

We never got to express our love outwardly and that always hurt me. It continues to hurt me now. I know it isn't your fault. I dread to think what would have happened to us if we had ever been discovered. I am not sure your mother would have been so forgiving as last time and I am sure she wouldn't have cared if Clai had gone a lot further than just tying me to a tree and beating me up a little.

One of the worst nights for me was the evening your mother brought Joquium to dinner. I thought I was going to die when she came to me and told me to lay out the best cutlery because she had someone special coming. She was excited and couldn't help but babble to me about the fact that she was trying to set you up with that arrogant officer.

You had known nothing about it until she surprised you with him at dinner. Of course you had to keep up pretences. There was no reason in anybody's eyes why you should not take an interest in the men your mother might parade in front of you.

I was serving drinks again that evening and had to watch you sit there and flirt with him to appease your mother.

"And guess what vehicle I'm driving now?" was the final straw for me. I had stood by, topping up his glass and bringing him out his food, as he had bragged about his military career, his house, his chef and anything else he could think of. I watched you sit there and smile politely. I saw how smitten your mother was with the idea of her daughter being with an esteemed officer who was by her own reckoning, 'dashing to look at'.

The bragging question regarding his car was accompanied by a conceited click of the fingers in my general direction and a point towards his glass signalling that he wanted me to top it up for him. I don't know if it was his cocky sense of superiority and haughtiness that made me lose my temper or having to watch him slobber all over you, but I knew I needed to bring an end to the evening. So I did the only thing in my power. I knocked his drink down his front.

He blurted out something which I have since come to learn was an extreme string of obscenities in Holiterian. You bit your lip to stifle a laugh and it reminded me of the way you bite it when we are together in bed and that thought carried me blissfully unaware through the immediate onslaught that followed; he stood up and began punching me. He cracked me in the ribs first and then attempted to pummel me straight in the face. I blocked it. I made no attempt to fight back but I wasn't prepared to let him have every hit.

He got in a few good hits. I took one to the chin which made me fly backwards but I quickly pulled myself up again. I knew that by standing up again I was allowing him the opportunity to hit me once more but I was determined to keep coming back because I knew it was the most insolent thing I could do. It worked. Every time I staggered myself back into an upright position he tried harder to keep me down. He threw himself into my attack with his fists and his feet and finally, a head butt.

You were screaming. You had never seen a fight before and you hated to see me getting hurt. Your mother hated to see you upset by the violence and the sight of my blood and she screamed, "For goodness sake, someone stop him!" So I did.

One swift punch to his face and he fell to the floor.

You and your mother stood there in absolute silence. The realisation of what I had done hit me then. I, a human, had knocked a Holiterian to the floor; and not just a Holiterian but a Holiterian officer nonetheless.

Klijia rushed in but it was all over by the time he had.

"You. To my office. Now!" Chi Atarah commanded pointing at me. Her eyes were cold.

"Mother, he only did as you asked..." I heard your voice, sweet as sugar, fill my ears as you pleaded my case for me and I headed towards her office.

I stood there, waiting outside the door and listened to time ticking by on the large clock in the hallway. Usually that clock marks the time that we are together and it always flies by far too quickly. This time, however, I was alone and the clock was marking my passage to punishment. I prayed, harder than I have ever prayed before, that I wouldn't be sent away.

I knew I could take any physical punishment they want to throw at me but the one thing that I couldn't stand was to be sent back to the compound and to never see you again.

I heard her heels click-click-clicking up the corridor.

"You have a guardian angel tonight," she informed me.

I looked at her confused.

"My daughter has made the very good point that the man was a... now, what was the word she used? Oh yes, that was it, he was an 'egotistical cock' and that you were merely following my orders. Newly rich, that's the problem. He can be as pretty as he likes but there is something about them. They can't help but boast. And blowing one's own trumpet, as you humans like to say, is never good."

She paused and I felt like there was an expectation on me to speak, "Ma'am," I said. It was neither question nor statement.

She went on, "I am telling you that you are free to go."

I stood there for a moment dazed. I had punched a Holiterian officer to the floor and somehow you had managed to talk your mother out of punishing me. I began to wonder if I truly did have a guardian angel. I had managed to get away with something that should probably have been punishable by death.

"You are already black and blue. I think you have been punished enough. Besides, you let him hit you like a rag doll until I gave the order to have him stopped. My daughter makes a compelling case."

"Thank you, Ma'am."

And that evening you came to me to clean up my face and plant a tender kiss on everyone of my cuts and bruises. And I thanked you in every way I knew how.

Chapter Five – Finding a Secret

Yesterday morning, we were woken in a panic, as we realised we had overslept and it was seven o'clock. The household was up and moving about and someone was knocking on my door.

I got up and answered it. My light was still off so I was blinded by the light from above as I opened the door and it streamed in. All I could see as I rubbed my eyes sleepily was a large, dark outline, looming in the middle of the brilliant, white sunlight.

"What the hell are you still doing in here? It is seven o'clock, you should have been downstairs half an hour ago and I don't have time for this today with everything else going on!"

"What's going on, sir?"

"What's going on? I will tell you what's going on! Clai has just gone in to check on Esmella and she isn't in her room. Her bed hasn't been slept in! That is what is going on!" he sounded increasingly irate as his speech went on. Although I am sure if you had not been standing just two feet away from him and in plain view of me, I might have been inclined to sound just as panic-stricken as he was.

It dawned on me that it was probably expected of me to react in just the same way.

"Oh no!" I said mustering as much concern as I thought appropriate for the occasion, "Does anybody have any idea where she has gone?"

"No. And everyone is out looking. You would do well to do the same. The Chi is in a terrible state. She won't take kindly to you if you don't seem to be helping!"

I turned around and picked up my clothes. He shut the door and left me to get dressed in the darkness. I threw my clothes on as quickly as I could and felt you sidle up behind me. You slid your arm up under my shirt, stoked my chest and brushed your thumb over my nipple. I turned around and kissed you passionately. I tried to pull away and you pulled me back to kiss you again. "I have to go and find you," I smiled.

"Well I hope you succeed," you told me.

"And you had better think of an amazing excuse as to where you have been when you turn up!"

"I'm sure I will, don't worry," you winked at me.

I kissed you once more and then rushed upstairs and into the light again.

It would have appeared odd if someone had walked past and seen my light shining out from around the door, so I left you there in the dark to come up with your plan. I was just heading down the corridor on the first floor when your mother came out of her office. Her eyes were bloodshot and she had clearly been crying.

"Ma'am, if you may permit me to speak?" I asked.

"Of course," she said.

"I am sure she will turn up soon- you have the best men on the whole planet here to keep her safe. I am sure she will be back soon wondering what all the fuss is for."

"Thank you," she said to me and squeezed my arm. "You're a good man."

I was shocked. This was perhaps the first nice thing your mother had ever said to me. She must have been really worried about you.

I had just resumed walking when she called me back. "I have been trying to read through the notes on some of her handhelds," she explained, "but I just can't focus. Can I give them to you to read? I need to see if there are any clues as to where she might be."

"I'm not sure," I stammered, "are you sure I would be the best person for the job?"

"Of course. You know to keep any secrets." She gave me a cheeky smile and added, "It's hardly like you would blackmail me. I could simply have you killed."

I laughed nervously because she sounded like she was joking, but at the same time, what she had said was brutally honest. She could simply have me killed.

I agreed to do it and left with the intention of taking them but not bothering to read them. After all, I knew where you were and I knew you were safe. So I took them and went and sat in the library in order to appear busy. In reality I sat there and thought about how amazing you are and how complete my life feels with you. You are the first person who has made me feel like the world is still a beautiful place. You brighten up my days and make it worth going on living.

I suddenly realised there was a possibility of someone else still reading through your handhelds if I should not come up with anything and you didn't return soon. I began to panic that there might be something on there to incriminate us. So I opened it up.

A large holographic projection appeared before me. There was nothing very exciting there. I flicked through everything. I had to smile as I deleted a page on which you had written, 'Mrs Esmella and Mr José Holfenstoff. You had doodled our images on there and there was something so sweet and ingenuous about it that reminded me of all the reasons why I love you.

I couldn't leave it there in your files as much as I would have loved to. It was too great of a risk to both of us. I committed it to my memory before deleting it for you. Then I continued to scroll through your documents. I got through the first two handhelds without any problems, but the third one was different.

I had just started to scroll through and it very quickly became apparent that it wasn't your handheld I was looking at. These documents were the official business documents of the Chi. I was about to put it down when one particular title caught my eye. It was titled The Truth and classified as highly confidential. Unlike everything else on there it was password protected. My curiosity got the better of me and I desperately wanted to know what it said.

It took me a long time to get into it, as I was no expert at cracking passwords. Luckily, I am an expert on you and you are your mother's favourite thing. So I managed to work out the password based on that.

That is when the document that you have just read came up.

I went through a range of emotions as I read it. Your mother has so many secrets. She has denied you of your right to a father and lied to you about your heritage. She has covered for a man who brought endless death and destruction to my planet. And worse of all, she finished it so abruptly! She ended it like it was a conclusion-like the compounds were a happily ever after ending for us.

Like us, she had been having a secret affair. Her affair was with your father and not the man you have been led to believe was your father. She claimed to love him yet she callously killed him in cold blood. I would never, for any reason, ever be able to murder you and I know in my heart that you would never be able to hurt me either. What sort of a person kills the one they love? I began to wonder whether she might have it in her to kill you too. I couldn't bring myself to leave you unprotected from her. It seems impossible to imagine, but what if you ever discovered something that jeopardised her power? Javari was in the process of proposing to her when she stabbed him. Surely he couldn't have thought her capable of doing it to him either?

Of all the people she wrote about, Amelia stuck in my mind the most. She was brutally murdered at the hands of Holiterians simply for having information. Now I found myself in the very same situation.

More than anything, I wanted to talk to you about this. But you were the last person I could talk to. So I acted alone.

I had been sat in the library, tearing my hair out as I tried to plan my next course of action. I tried to think what my mother would say or do. She was the one who was an expert at scheming. She had the mind for it. I wasn't sure I did, but I just had to engage with it.

So I sat thinking and working out different scenarios in my mind. I could easily hand it back and pretend I had never seen it. My fate would have been safer that way. By admitting to the knowledge I held and acting upon it, I knew I would run the risk of meeting the same fate as Amelia.

I thought again of my parents. I have never told you before but I was not their first and only son. There was a boy born before me. My parents are reluctant to talk about him because it is too painful. Occasionally my father will muse that he wished it had been him instead.

My mother had at times begun to open up to me about him before breaking down and clamming up again. His name was Sebastiano. Everyone called him Seb. He had been two years old when the explosions had occurred and, like my parents, had survived. Unfortunately, at such a tender age, the radiation had been too much for his tiny body to handle. He looked sickly, developed a hacking cough, brought up blood and then finally, as cancer raged through his fragile body, he passed away, just two months later.

He died in the arms of my mother. She believes the only blessing was that he passed before they were found by Holiterians and rounded up into the prisons. She is glad he was never sent there. Although it was the longest, most painful two months of her life watching her infant child be consumed by the radiation, at least her and my father were with him to comfort him. In the hospitals, she dreads to think what might have happened.

And here I was, with all that knowledge, contemplating putting myself into a situation where they could end up suffering the death of their second child too. Emotion began to cloud my vision and fell heavy on my chest.

That was when I was interrupted by the jubilant noise confirming that you had been found alive and well. I took a deep breath, straightened myself up and went out into the hall; Klijia was there.

"She's found?" I asked him.

"Just returned now."

"Safe?"

"Yes. Forbidden to leave her room. Clai is on guard at the door."

I never did learn what excuse you had given. Whatever it had been I knew there was no chance of seeing you that evening.

In a way, as much as I would have loved to have spent another night with you, it was probably for the best that it didn't happen. It gave me the time that I needed to get my head straight and formulate what I was going to do next.

I didn't sleep at all. I had never hurt anyone before and as much as I hated your mother, she had never been horrible to me on a personal level. It was hard to marry the two images in my mind: the woman who was capable of giving orders for brutality towards my people versus the woman who had brought me into her home as a slave but offered me a reasonable standard of living and shown me several acts of kindness.

I had to push my own memories of your mother out of my mind. I had to focus on the version of her that I was less familiar with. She had killed a man using her own hands. She had ordered the deaths of hundreds of my people. She may not have killed them herself but she was responsible for the actions of her men. She may as well have taken a knife and stabbed each one individually the way she did to your father.

I allowed rage to boil through me. I needed to own it in order to do what I knew in my heart I needed to do today.

Chapter Six – Assassination

I killed her.

I put on some gloves and went to your mother's office under the pretence of handing back your handhelds.

She looked up and smiled at me when she saw me come in, "Oh, thanks for that. Just pop them there, thank you." It was one of those moments of kindness where I doubted she was truly bad but then I reminded myself of the things she had written and it brought my fury back to the surface.

I thought of all the things she has done over the years to you, to my people and to her own people as well. The fire burned savagely in my heart and I moved over to her and put my hands around her neck. It happened in an instant.

Her skin felt warmer than I expected; I think I was hoping it would be as cold as her heart. The warmth made me hesitate for a moment. It made it all seem so real. I couldn't risk giving her the time to scream so I closed my hands together.

The veins that ran through her neck bulged as I squeezed tightly to cut off her air flow. Her beautiful eyes began to bulge in their sockets. In spite of my smaller size, adrenaline made me strong and she flapped around like a fish on a hook. She continued to thrash for what felt like an eternity but no noise could escape her pretty little mouth.

She reminded me of you so much that I wanted to stop but I had passed the point of no return. She needed to be stopped and I had the power to do it.

I gave her a short, sharp shake and her body went still.

Nobody rushed in as I feared they might. I had made hardly any noise as I committed my horrible deed. Nobody would suspect me. After all, I had been part of your household for years. I may have been human but I think it was forgotten sometimes.

I had never killed a person before. I wondered, at first, how you knew when they were really dead, so I continued to hold on for a long, long time. Then her body began to feel cold and stiff as the blood stopped moving. She was so still and peaceful. I removed my hand and saw the dark marks around her neck where my hands had been. That was the moment when I knew for definite what I had done. She was really, truly dead.

I took off my gloves, threw them into my back pocket and raised the alarm, "Help! Somebody! Come quick- something is wrong!"

People came sprinting into her office and stood there in shock at the body on the floor before them.

I looked at her too. I had killed her.

Then you came in.

Grief broke you in two and you fell to the floor screaming. I longed to rush to you and pick you up but I knew I couldn't. I let Clai and Klijia pick you up. I looked at you but you didn't see me or anyone else. You were blinded by the tears pouring down your face.

And I felt terrible because it was me who killed her. And I knew that today I would give you this and your heart would break all over again.

Chapter Seven – Today

I started writing this the night before last. Since I committed my crime, I have spent my time completing this letter. It was imperative I had it finished by this morning because I wanted you to read this as soon as possible. I know that you have to attend a meeting today. I also know that in the meeting you will be given the title of Chi, the title that you deserve. I know that you might never forgive me for what I have done. You needed all of this information before your meeting.

In writing you this letter, I have betrayed my own people. I have told you our plans to look for weakness in your leadership and the human desire to take over our planet again. This will probably mean you will continue to keep them downtrodden and in slavery.

In my actions, I have betrayed you. I knew all last night that killing your mother might just be the one thing you could never forgive me for, no matter how despicable her actions. So I have potentially ruined all of the relationships on this Earth that I hold dearest to me.

I am truly sorry for the pain that you have suffered but I am afraid I can never be sorry for killing your mother.

*

From Esmella-

My Darling, José,

Forgive me for sending this to you in the hands of a messenger. I wanted to speak to you myself but today security has locked everything down. Until I know your response to this letter, I cannot bring you to my side.

You were right; it was agony the moment that you killed my mother and again when I read her story and yours too. It was too much for me. All the blood on the hands of my people is blood on my hands. Hearing of all the hardship you have suffered in silence shattered me.

By allowing me to read the truth, all of the memories that I have of my mother are destroyed. They are besmirched by her wicked deeds. That doesn't mean I am not glad to know. Ignorance may be bliss but when I am to lead a planet, knowledge is vital.

And my heart continues to break every moment I think of the life you kept a secret from me. The life you endured on the compound, the life your friends and family continue to endure, it is traumatising. I wonder how I could have been so blind as to live alongside it all these years and yet never have seen it. I wonder how I could have looked at the broken spirit behind your eyes and not have realised it was so damaged. I only saw the light of your love.

I feel as if I have grown up years in these past 24 hours.

Malachi, who is like a grandfather to me, is now like a stranger. I can't imagine how I can even begin to punish him for his role in all of this. I wonder whether I would have been courageous enough to have acted as you did if I had found my mother's letters first. Could I have killed her by my own hands, as she deserved? I am not sure I could.

I cannot foresee a way of unpicking the mess of the compounds. Your people are furious, rightly so, and if I give them the freedom they deserve then they will fight and revolt against me. Although I am Holiterian, is my home. If I am banished from here then I have nowhere familiar. If I keep your people locked up and punished for being human then I am no better than my mother.

I find myself in a dire position here with nobody I can trust and seemingly no solution.

Honestly, in the past hour since reading this, I have contemplated suicide. There are no heirs after me though and that would leave this planet open to anyone corrupt and violent enough to take it. If it is possible, the situation here could get even worse. Imagine if someone with the mindset of Abram came to power. Those awful hospitals could be reinstated. The limited freedom of the humans could be revoked.

Whilst worrying about all this, I remembered something I had read somewhere a long time ago in a forgotten language of this planet. Amor Vincit Omnia. Love conquers all.

My mother spoke in her speech to the people of 'Earthers'. Holiterians and humans as one. This is an idea that has never materialised. I have never heard this term since. It is an idea that would tie us together and has the potential to bring us some sense of peace.

To show my commitment to healing the wounds, I will clear this entire planet of radiation. I will encourage people to go off and resettle in different locations worldwide. There is enough space on this planet for everyone alive to settle here. I will send medical teams from my planet around the world. In exchange for the antibodies from the human placentas, I will offer our cure for the cancers still rampant since the explosions. I will set our men to finding alternatives to assist our immunity that doesn't involve dependence on humans. Anything is possible.

You wrote of already losing your family through your betrayal to them and I am potentially about to ask you to betray them further. You said you would do anything for me; are you prepared to marry me? Because I am proposing we allow our love to attempt to conquer these problems before us. We can stand before the people as wife and husband and as equals.

We will lead by example and give them the better equal life they ask for. And if neither side approves, well then they can all unite against us together. As their common enemy, we will be the ones to bring them together in our deaths.

At least then we give them the choice. A life where we try to rebuild love and harmony together or a vicious fight in which there are likely to be no survivors and no winners.

I love you more than anyone. So I guess what I am asking you, José, is: will you marry me?

ACKNOWLEDGEMENTS

With thanks to my fabulous family and friends. Without your support and encouragement, I wouldn't be sat here with a finished novel. I apologise for the months you lost me to my laptop! To my readers- I thank you for your patience and unwavering enthusiasm in spite of the never-ending supply of 'new versions' of each chapter. Special thanks also to my copy-editor, whose background in science and unfaltering attention to detail helped me to refine my ideas.